In a Shallow Grave

Other Books by James Purdy

ARBOR HOUSE
New York

In a Shallow Grave

by James Purdy

For Edward G. Hefter,
Robert Helps,
and George Andrew McKay.

In a Shallow Grave

"WHAT you will need now you are about to be separated from the Army," my captain had told me as I was picking up my mustering-out pay, "is what in the days of my grandfather they called a valet or maybe a hired man. Unless of course you want to stay in the Vets' hospital, which you have more than every right to . . . But you will need someone to watch over you now . . ."

I didn't think about a valet and/or hired man until I was back home in Virginia for a week or so. Somehow all I thought about the first few days was how many birds there were singing in the early or premorning hours, I never heard such a fuss. I thought some too about my parents who had died whilst I was in service, and I thought about somebody else whom I am coming to very presently. I felt also a certain kind of angry satisfaction, if not gratitude, for all the money I had on hand, not to speak of some my uncle had willed me, I say angry or grim satisfaction owing to the fact that both the captain and me knew there would be no valet, hired man, even slave who would want to come and stay with *me*, not to mention eat with or touch me, for I may as well explain at once that owing to my war injuries which took place near the South China Sea, my appearance is such that anybody's stomach is turned at the sight, enough to make him throw up, if not to faint.

I kept sort of grinning thinking over the captain's advice about valets and servants and hired men, but as another soldier who was being mustered out at the same time as me had quipped, "*When you can't even find anybody to shine your shoes anymore, let alone somebody to watch over you.*"

But behind all these practical considerations and worries, there was this flitting dim thought never absent but never put into words at this time, that down the road about two mile was living Widow Rance, who had been, though this seems a thousand years ago and must surely have passed out of her mind entirely, my childhood sweetheart.

But though I thought of her every moment asleep or awake, under the sound of all those bird choristers, it finally wasn't my lifelong crush on her that made me hold my breath with panic but what was I to do with the little that was left of myself.

The Army doc, just before he signed my papers, had said, "Although your skin bears a total disfigurement from your war injuries, you ought to bear in mind, despite your outward appearance you have a wonderful fine and strong bone structure, and it is the bones that are the real measure of a man's bearing and good looks."

In the darkness now sometimes after my return I would take out a large hand mirror and look at myself as if searching for the bones that he had said I should be so proud of. By moonlight it is true, I looked sort of almost normal, the scars, gashes, and discoloration sort of melting into the night . . . Yes, I needed a servant, I kept returning to this. No woman would take the job, that's certain, though I would have preferred one. It would have to be not only a man, but a young one, for already you see I had my plan, and I would run his legs off. So I put some notices in the local papers advertising for him, for I knew then that I would court the Widow Rance through these letters I was going to write to her.

But it was maybe my greatest sorrow since I was hurt so bad in the war when the ads started to be answered and the applicants began coming in person. I had never interviewed anybody before, and always been the one to have to answer all the questions, and here I was about to ask these young men if they would care to accept employment. But there were few questions asked, let me tell you, and almost no answers, for all the young men acted the same way, that is they took one look, and their gorge started to rise, and they would strain and cough, wanting to vomit as they looked over at me. After that, they would get up, knocking over a stool or taboret somewhere, some mumbling *"No thanks, buddy,"* or *"Sorry about all your trouble over there."* One even started to shake hands with me, but when he saw the disfigurement had reached as far down as my fingertips he thought better of it, and hiked out faster than the ones who had left almost as soon as they caught sight of me.

I am glad the doc has left me a generous medicine cabinet, for as soon as an applicant had retched and knocked over the furniture and hurried out, I would take more than my usual handful of pills.

I presided over fifty acres here, left me by my grandfather, who in turn had it from his father. Nearby is the ocean, which sort of follows my moods, that is sometimes even when the sky is bright he thunders and thumps and howls and even cries like a little child. And speaking of crying, my doc says my injuries have not really damaged my lachrymal glands, but I think on this score as on many others, he must have blundered, for I cannot weep, and if I start to I feel a great pain in these said glands, like there were sharp rocks or millstones being drawn through raw nerves.

I don't know what I would do without the ocean, come to think of it.

At first I wrote down in diary form my thoughts, but I burned them one morning. The pages from my diary though began with one sentence which from then on seemed to float through the air like smoke rings from a billboard cigarette, *I am the color now of mulberry juice.*

It's as though any chair I sat on was a red-hot stove, my bed is like ground glass, and even when walking, from my scalp down to my big toe I feel I am on fire . . . "*It is memory,*" said the docs, "*you have recovered from your war injuries, it is your memory which keeps you in pain, learn to forget and you will be well again.*"

But if I do have memory, like they say it is buried to the core the earth, for I really have trouble recollecting one day from the next.

The "interviews" and the "advertisements" for hired help took all of a year. Even now I can see the long line of young men who came to apply for a job nobody could want.

I thought once, and wrote it out on a scrap sheet from a ledger, *The lowest slave in the world wouldn't accept the job of tending me if he was to starve to death.*

Only it finally "came" to me in the night that somebody desperate *was* going to apply, and as soon as this thought warned me of his coming, I got sort of quiet even for me, and slept.

There was a little old pump-organ upstairs, and I used to go up and pump it and play folk songs on it, and even sing, but it only made me more uncomfortable in my head, for the purpose of folk songs whether they admit it or not is to get you to weep.

None who came, then, as applicants could bear the sight of me, all turned aside to retch or to groan or to sit down too faint to stand, and would beg for a glass of water. The hired girl I had at this time used to let them in, and almost as quick let them out. One applicant who lingered a little longer than the others while the girl waited at the door to allow him to leave opined that when winter came he feared the house would be too skeletal and thin to keep the big winds and ocean blasts out. I nodded, as cold was the last thing on my mind, and I reminded him that in the summer it is breezy and cool here when the rest of the country is sweltering and broiling.

All the time the applicants was coming and going I was thinking if only I could lay my head in her (Widow

Rance's) lap, my brow and brain would get cool, my
lachrymal glands would work, and I would be my old self.
 Your old sweet self.

Now as to the applicants for this job. I drew up a list of
their duties on the same scraps from the ledger on which I
finally wrote down the story of my life. They were to sit
with me, fetch me a glass of water so I could swallow my
pills, occasionally or even frequently when my feet went
cold they would rub them and the skin over my heart, and
see I got three square meals a day, even though I didn't
even want one, and finally read to me, though I was too
nervous to sit still to hear them. They would read to me as
I paced up and down the sitting room, or wherever.

So I got quite handy at shooting those questions to the
applicants, while neither of us looked at the other: *"Can
you prepare simple food? Like say heat already prepared
soup, boil coffee, rub my feet when my attack comes on
and the flesh above my heart, and can you take letters to
the Widow Rance?"* (She had agreed to accept messages
from me through the offices of an intermediary.)

Each minute, each hour lasted an eternity. I am twenty-
six according to the back pages of the family Bible that lies

open over there to the Book of Second Samuel, but the handwriting should say twenty-six millennia, maybe. No medicine or new pharmaceutical can help when I look in the mirror. What age is that looking back at me in that antique glass decorated with painted nasturtiums on the surrounding wood, is he human, a man, some stray animal, who is looking back at me? Somebody I never met, nor knew, nor saw . . .

But to return to the duties of these applicants. They was to sit with me, fetch me a glass of water, and so on. But I said all this before, see how wrong the docs are about my memory.

The Widow Rance is twenty-eight but sometimes acts like some old rich woman of sixty. Of her two husbands (she was first married at sixteen), the first died in the same war I was in, then she remarried his brother a year after his death, he ditto went to war and died. She told everybody that was enough, she would not remarry. Oh yes I forgot, her babies both died, she had one each by the two brothers.

James Powell, my first hired applicant, gave me the distinct impression she hated me now, and only accepted the letters because I am a hero, but we will come to James Powell first.

I can kind of see him yet if I close one eye, if I close two he disappears on me, this first applicant. What makes me remember him at all may be only that he was the first.

He stood over me, I remember, like a barber and that made me jumpy. When he brought in my scrapple and eggs, he stood behind my head at the big pine table while I ate. Finally, after the second day, I said, *"James Powell, do you have to stand behind my head always? Go to the other end of the table, and stand with your hands along the seams of your trousers, head and nose slightly raised, eyes on . . . nothing. Is that clear?"*

Powell swallowed hard, I suppose with choler, and said it was.

I would eat the scrapple then but only in order to have the strength to bear my suffering for that day, as I have no taste for food.

"How old are you, Powell?"

"Would you mind calling me either by my Christian name or say *Mister* when you address me?"

"Of course, Mr. Powell. How old then are you?"

"Sixteen years and four months and two days."

"I never heard of anybody that age being called 'Mister.' " I said this so under my breath he may not have heard it.

"It's only fair to tell you, James," I began, but I could not remember what I was going to say to him, and got up from the table, spinning. He rushed over to me and held me under the armpits, and we walked that way to a large overstuffed sofa, and I sort of slipped from his arms onto it.

The routine after breakfast was interrupted then by this "spell" of mine—he was to have taken a letter I was writing to the Widow—for I had this strange feeling of ice beginning to flow from my feet and legs upwards like the poison hemlock reported by Socrates' pupil, on its way to my heart. I wanted to die, but I feared the experience of death itself.

His hands began rubbing my feet, for I guess, to give him his due, he understood my condition at that moment.

Despite my being took so bad, my mind was on having hurt his feelings by saying nobody his age could be called *Mister*, and considering how after all he was younger than me, a boy and a childlike one, though in some respects old and mean in his ways, I began to apologize to him somewhat profusely in order, I do believe, to keep my thoughts away from my possible death, but he was even more afflicted by my apologies, and got up in confusion and went over to a rocking chair and sat down, but kept his feet in such a position the chair would not rock with him.

"All right, I am sorry, Jim. I am sorry, Mr. Powell."

He broke down then and began to bawl. I am not exactly sure what he was bawling over, but I suppose everything.

The second part of the day began then, as I say, when we were interrupted by my "attack" by us going into the study and I would start writing a letter to Widow Rance.

James would take a pad and pencil (he claimed to know shorthand), and I would begin to dictate:

"Dearest and only Girl"

But after that I could think of nothing to say, and finally looking up and catching the expression on his face, I let out, "See here, Mr. Powell, I don't see why you act more miserable and more on a bed of hot coals than me."

He was looking down at his hands and especially his fingernails, and then it began to dawn on me a little bit what was bothering him, he did not like having to rub my feet to prevent the cold from going up and reaching my heart, that is he had a real distatste for having to touch the human foot. Well, the human foot is the real nigger of the human body, as my sergeant once said to me outside our tent, mistreated, bad-smelling even in the most elegant lady, deformed by footgear, unhappy by the burdens placed on it from the time you begin to toddle, and is the first part of the body (he was thinking of soldiers) to die.

I had never quite understood the sergeant's speech until James Powell maybe. But now *it all* came back to me in a rush, but I didn't care, I mean my coming death meant nothing to me, it was the fact I had never known joy in this world that seemed so terrible, mind you I didn't blame anybody or circumstances, but what I wondered suddenly was *had anybody known joy in this world, real joy?* I knew James Powell never had, there was no use asking him.

I had begun dictating my letter to Widow Rance, James' long, untrimmed fingernails making sounds on the yellow-lined paper:

Dear Widow Rance, All I meant to say when you granted me my last interview is that I am not spying on you at all when I stand so considerably hidden by the hollyhocks which I also understand are growing on another property than your own, I am standing partially hidden as I speak to you behind these tall plants only to spare you from being upset and/or affrighted by my changed aspect since we were schoolmates, for I understand my appearance causes you to be discomfited, at least James or Mr. Powell so informs me that you are unhappy when I do appear whether behind or in front of the hollyhocks . . .

"Stop!" the first applicant called out to me . . . "Stop, do you hear? You are making fun of me . . . I never reported anything you ever said to the Widow Rance."

I looked at him dumbfounded, because it was true, I did despise him, and was probably making fun of him in my heart. We certainly were not getting on.

"And these letters!" he cried, throwing his pencil to the floor. "Don't you understand Widow Rance has no use for . . . them. She never wants to hear from you again. She hates your letters!"

I slumped back in my chair, really done up at what he had said.

By the way, my name is Garnet Montrose. It is a name people stumble on, a fact I noticed in the first grade, at school dances (I was a great dancer, I think it is the one thing I did good, dance, I could dance all day or night to Kingdom Come, I lived at dance halls all the time before I was drafted, under the ballroom moving lights, you know, the little dappled specks of color and the girl with her young little breasts so neatly against my ribcage, well, maybe come to think of it I have known joy, my trouble then as now is I don't know what to do with the rest of my life). As I say, people stumble on hearing my name, the first name doesn't fit with the second, the first name, they feel, sounds like a girl's, and the second sounds to them too historical. In the Army most often as not they just called me by two nicknames which have, to tell the truth, always puzzled me, one was *Granite*, and the other was *Morose*, and at the beginning they used to joke and pun around the first nickname and say *"Don't let them take you for granite, soldier."* But now I am home I want only my own names used, but actually nobody calls me anything because nobody can see me to call me, you might say. I am more vague than the fog, and not even it seems to me as palpable as night.

Mr. Powell then really tore into me, he said I was an ignorant, arrogant, half-assed plantation owner, and so on, and then he fled out of the house like it was afire, and I realized I would never see him more, and would have to put in ads all over again, on the long tiresome search for a nurse, bodyguard, or whichever to watch over somebody who didn't want to be among the land of the living even. Where would I find him, you tell me.

I looked over my file of letters to Widow Rance as I was cooling off from my battle with Mr. Powell, letters I keep faded copies of. I heard secondhand from somebody, maybe Mr. Powell himself, that the Methodist minister had paid the widow a visit, and said to her, *"Just keep the letters from him coming, he means you no harm."*

The other thing that annoyed the applicants about me was this, they did not like what one smartass called my metaphysical speeches. I know no metaphysics or philosophy, I don't know anything. But I would talk on two topics which are simply reality to me, joy and the meaninglessness of death. Is there joy in this world for anybody, and has death any meaning? They would, as one of the early applicants phrased it, like to foam at the mouth when I did these discussions.

None of the applicants liked anything I did or said and I will not even bother to describe the early ones, none liked anything about me as I say until, well, you wait now.

There was at least four applicants before my favorite came. And let me warn you, I do not believe he was from this world. I believe he was sent by the Maker of All Things perhaps, if such exists. I do not say that he brought me total joy, but he was the ideal applicant.

But just before he resigned, packed, and lit out, James Powell had sat down, and said a thing which considerably lightened my heart. "Garnet," he began, in that pained cautious weary-with-sin look preachers often put on, "Widow Rance reads your letters and keeps them."

And before I could ask any details concerning this hurricane sentence, he was gone. I ran out to the big road after him, but his old jalopy had already carried him away. I stood in the big road for quite a spell, and some people going by then in a big car with a New York license took one look at me and said, *"Where in hell are we if they are all going to look like him now?"*

These remarks about my appearance still hurt me at this stage of my life, but not like they did when I first come out of the Army, when people would stop on the street in Washington, D.C., and scream or retch, and I would go back to the Army hospital and groan and clench my hands and tear my shoelaces out of my shoes. Usually the doc was watching me by the door, and would repeat the same thing, *"These things pass, Garnet, and you are in the land of the living, remember, while all your buddies are gone."*

But Doc is not marked with the coating of death as I am, and my buddies are at least all safe-dead, while I have been allowed to live but with the appearance of one from the under-kingdom.

"Doc," I said, now that I had him engaged in conversation, "how do I look to other folks, do you think?"

Doc give me his speech then again about bone structure, height, posture, and my hair, yes, isn't this sort of a joke too on me, my hair is the kind of blond hair that looks like corn tassel, and in the right light looks almost white, so that I remember my first-grade teacher had said, "*You have hair a girl would die for*," and whilst everything else turned the color of mulberries, my hair was untouched by when I was blown up in the war, and so it has made me look even more outlandish.

My education had stopped at the eighth grade because I was incorrigible, but I had what my mother said was the bad habit of reading, but I always read books nobody else would turn more than a page of, and my knowledge is and was all disconnected, unrelated, but the main book I always kept to even after my explosion-accident was an old old one called *Book of Prophecies*. From it comes my only knowledge of mankind now. I read and have read to me, however, nearly everything, my house is all books and emptiness.

But James Powell's words stayed with me—I have said this before—like big smoke rings from the cigarette billboard ads. I could see and taste his words,

WIDOW RANCE READS YOUR LETTERS AND KEEPS THEM.

I hurried to the spinet desk, I put the dip-pen in the violet ink, I praised the Lord almost, though my Lord you must understand I see as a kind of doglike man with a sad face Who watches the gate here, He never says anything to me, He knows my suffering, and He knows that my buddies are not as dead as I, and He knows I must walk upon the earth for a spell before going down into the total mulberry night. Anyhow, I wrote then this:

> My Darling Girl,
> All that I ask is that you allow me to tell you you are on my heart and mind. We will never meet again unless you should go so far as to invalidate your first edict, that I was never to darken your door, never to speak to you, and if possible never appear before you in light or darkness. I will respect your wishes, but allow me to write to you, I cannot say what is on my mind or you would think I pitied myself, the great sin according to the Big World. I do not pity myself, but I know I am as bad off as a man might ever get and yet I cling to life in you. Allow me this.
>
> Your servant,   Garnet Montrose

There at the door like sent by providence was the egg-man Edgar Doust. He had the practice of never looking at me even indirectly. He counted out the eggs, or the chicken wings, sometimes said, *"Garnet, we have pullet eggs today, want any?"*

"And milk, Edgar," I would remind him, "you always forget the milk. I have a commission I'd like to ask of you, Edgar," I said, for I spoke half in Virginia language now and half in language out of the *Book of Prophecies*, and also occasionally from the *History of the Papacy*, which I forgot to mention maybe because it is the least favorite of my books.

"And that would be?" Edgar Doust inquired.

"As soon as I lick the envelope," I said, hurrying back to the spinet desk and putting my letter to her in it and then licking harder, "*Would you deliver this message to the Widow Rance?*"

"*Let me tell you something,*" Edgar began.

He was a short, stubby man, came only to my breast-bone, for as the doc always said when I felt I was too much a goblin to be counted among mankind, "*Remember your height, Garnet. You have the great bone structure of the English-speaking race . . .*" (I am six foot four in my stocking feet).

"Now see here," Edgar was going on, starting to touch my shoulder and then drawing back suddenly. "You have scared that poor woman nearly into her grave. She has a fear of you that is killing her. She may even pull up stakes and move away."

"No, Edgar," I began proudly. "Let me tell you something. I have news that puts your cocky little know-it-all palaver to shame . . ."

"What's in this letter then that I am to bear?" Edgar Doust wanted to know, drawing back.

"Nothing anybody need be ashamed of having writ or to receive," I tossed back at him.

"All right then," he said, starting to saunter off, and I handed him his money for the poultry, milk, and eggs. "But if I hear you has put anything low-down in this letter, and I am the bearer of it . . . watch out!"

I am in such an absentminded distant frame of mind that people often say goodbye to me or give me whole long speeches and then leave and I haven't heard what they said at all or noticed they have even left. Then suddenly I come out from this brown study and I am sitting looking at vacant chairs. When young men are not reading to me or rubbing my feet, I sometimes say aloud the names of my buddies who were blown up with me. Being Virginians their names are all sort of like mine, names city people say they find odd or made-up when here they are the real names of this country. Still they are hard, I guess, to pronounce for outsiders.

But Widow Rance, though she loathed and despised me and would rather meet an army of black spiders than see me behind the hollyhocks, here she had give me a reprieve by her kind words issued through that conceited snot James Powell. He done that one good thing anyhow, given me a shred of hope. Though dead I could tell one person some of my thoughts even though she forbade me to tell them face to face as she would had I been counted among the living.

———————————————

It must have been the middle of June, because the bob-whites were making such a fuss in the woods as it was their mating time, and they were hollering to one another, and this black fellow about eighteen came up and rapped on the screen door. I don't know whether he had heard of me or not, evidently not really for he started to speak as I stood slightly shaded by the screen, holding the *Book of Prophecies* in my right hand, and commencing to lift the latch and saying, "What you want?"

He started to speak again, his tongue moving and his lips twisting, but no words came out the second time either.

"Mrs. Pettison wonders if you wants the goats," he finally got out after looking every which way when he spoke.

"Why, what does she want to give them to me for?" I inquired.

"Old Mr. Pettison is dead, and she can't keep them no more," he replied. "She gonna move to Richmond."

"What are you, their hired man?"

I opened the door and let him in.

We was in the kitchen now, if I recollect accurately, and I invited him to sit down partly, I think, so he wouldn't fall down. There was a sliver in my finger that was causing me no end of pain, and having laid down the *Book of Prophecies* on the tablecloth, I was trying to work it out with a tiny pair of scissors. When I quit looking in his direction to get this sliver out he got easier with me. I heard him tell me his name after a while, Quintus Pearch.

"Why I know your folks, Quintus."

Just then we both looked up at the same time and saw the goats had come up on the back porch and were looking through the screen.

"Why there's five of the buggers, Quintus," I said. "I don't know, I never kept goats before . . . What I'm really looking for," and I studied him a little bit out of the corner of an eye, "is a sort of helper around here for myself . . ."

Before I knew what had happened, he was working that sliver out from my finger without being asked.

"Mrs. Pettison's niece Miss Ledsam must have been the one sent you about the goats, wasn't it?" I went on talking to keep from screaming as he took out the sliver, for my flesh, you see, all falls away at the slightest pressure, exposing the bones.

He showed me the sliver now caught in the blades of the scissors.

I thanked him, and then hurried to get out, "Excuse me, but can you read?"

"I read, Mr. Montrose."

"What do you read?"

"Anything printed I can run my eye over."

"Can you read . . . aloud?"

"How do you mean that?" Quintus inquired.

"I mean, if I was to put a book in your hands and I sat on a chair, see, when I'm not well, especially come winter, would you sit and face me and read out loud to me?"

Quintus thought about this, and then I rushed into the next room, and took down a dusty volume of history and put it in his hands and said, "Read this, why don't you, any place at all will do."

Quintus held the book as if it was as alive as one of the young goats outside, that is the book seemed to struggle in his hands and want down, but he began nonetheless to read very neatly and fluidly from this book writhing in his strong fingers:

"You shed the blood of my brother on the banks of the Mississippi twenty years ago, and what then? I am here today, thank God, to vindicate the principles baptized in his blood."

I took the book from his hands, just as it was about to wiggle out from his grasp, and put it down on the cloth.

"I could pay you good, Quintus," I said after complimenting him in my mind on the way he could read. "I'm most desperate for company in the bargain . . . Can you rub cold feet, by the way?"

"I couldn't leave Mama," Quintus finally said. "She most bedridden."

"Aha . . . Why don't you want the goats?" I sort of turned the subject.

"Well," Quintus stumbled around, "we don't want the care of animals now."

"Well, I want the goats," I told him, looking out through the screen.

One was only a small kid, and I went out on the back porch and picked it up and brought it in. "I want the goats," I said again, holding the little fellow to me. Its fur was quite damp, and I asked Quintus to reach me a cloth and I wiped him dry. "Why didn't I think of having goats before?" I said.

I looked up suddenly and saw that expression on his face that everybody eventually gets when they look at me. We both looked down immediately at the floor.

"Do you find me so sickening to look at, Quintus?" I said throatily after a long pause.

31

"No, sir."

"You read good, Quintus . . . Would you read for me in the evening, or maybe rub my feet when they get to be on the ice-cold order?"

"I could come in the evenings, after I tend to Mama . . ."

"I'll pay you good, Quintus."

"Tell you what," Quintus began, standing up, "I could come over most days in the P.M., and do your chores."

"I don't want chores, Quintus. I want somebody to read to me and rub my feet."

He looked discontented and troubled.

"Well, don't come then, Quintus, don't come . . . I have to have my feet rubbed, though . . . I'm not trying to . . . you know . . ."

"I'll come at four today if you want me to," he all of a sudden blurted out, and rose.

"By the way, do you know Widow Rance, Quintus, who lives down the road?"

"Oh yes."

"You're a familiar face to her and all?"

"Widow Rance knows me, knows Mama, yes . . ."

"Because the other thing I might ask you, and I don't know why I forgot it, for it's way and beyond the most important thing, is to deliver and fetch letters . . . Well, we'll talk later . . . Till the P.M. then, Quints . . ."

It's like I disremember Quintus' ever coming on that P.M., though, but of course he come, and was to come and go again and was regular about a lot of things, but he didn't have had to come in a way, because *somebody else* did.

Oh, there was other applicants too. I can't begin to remember all of them, though I have wrote their names down on a slip of paper I keep in the family Bible, but none of them was right, and Quintus might have been too right, but you see this other person came, and that's the real occasion of me writing down on, slip by slip of paper, this diary in my mind.

Let me try to say it like this. I thought he was a will-o'-the-wisp when I first laid eyes on him, for we have plenty of them here in the early summer. I had gone to let the goats sleep in one of the little sheds we used to have for sheep in the winter, the goats were making a fuss, I guess, at their strange surroundings, and I paused, after having locked them in, and I looked out toward the ocean, which was still as flat sand, and I saw this motionless something that looked like a light about maybe to go out.

"Who is that?" I said to this "appearance" which was now leaning on the pine tree as I spoke. "What are you about?" No answer.

I didn't need any sign about warning trespassers on my land because I was dreaded more than a hundred riflemen.

Had my appearance scared the daylights out of whoever was leaning against that tree? I walked slowly over the sloping ground to the hemlock tree. There he was, the trespasser and staring at me with his open blue eyes, with his hair even lighter than mine, and a face that was most winsome except he had, as I was later to understand, no front teeth, which only made him somehow more agreeable, at least younger looking.

"Are you an . . . applicant?" I inquired at last, as he merely stared in my direction.

"Go away," the trespasser finally spoke, and a moment later, "Can't you leave me be, mister?"

"Go away, huh?" I chewed my ire. "Do you realize you're on my property . . . ?"

"I'll get in a minute. Give me a chance to catch my breath . . ."

Just then he slipped and fell to one knee, and I instinctively reached down and lifted him up, and then he caught a full view of my face as I was bending over him and he let out a yell of horror. Before I knew what I had done I had struck him, and I don't think I have ever struck a man before except in self-defense in all my life, and I mean I really struck him, for the blow brought the blood.

He kept wiping off the blood and looking at it on his fingers, and paid no attention to my many apologies of *"I'm heartfelt sorry, I didn't mean to, don't know what come over me."*

Just then the smallest of the young goats, which had escaped from the shed where I put them, come wandering out and crying. The trespasser stooped down and began petting it.

"Well, what do you aim to do?" I questioned him at last, my anger sort of returning. "You can't just stand here . . .

Tell you what, I'll invite you in even though you say you ain't an applicant . . ."

He paid me no more attention, absorbed in his attentions with the kid.

Disgusted with him and his having made me lose control of myself I said, *"To hell with you then,"* and went inside.

I got all wrapped up after a bit in taking apart an old hall clock that had belonged to my grandfather, and forgot all about the incident in the pine grove.

I don't know how much time had slipped by, but I know it was dark, black dark out. I looked up from my sitting room where I was fixing the tiny wires of the clock and seen the trespasser standing at the kitchen screen door still holding the kid in his arms. We stared at one another through that long expanse of rooms as if he was looking at me from the entrance of the world to come.

Suddenly he reached to open the screen door and came inside with the goat.

"You can't bring no animal in here," I spoke sharply.

He paid no mind and sat down on the smallest kitchen chair with the kid in his lap. It had gone to sleep under his petting.

I came rushing then into the kitchen.

"You have a most irksome way of not answering questions," I said. "I asked you if you was an applicant and you didn't deign to answer."

"I ain't an applicant," he replied, saucy, through his missing front teeth.

"Where you from then, and what do you want?"

"Utah," he said after a deliberate hesitation.

Then for the first time he looked me straight in the face with his merciless wide-open sky-blue eyes, and then making a terrible sound, dropping the goat, he retched fearfully bending down trying desperately to vomit, but nothing coming up but a few strands of phlegm and water.

I left the kitchen and stumbled into the big front sitting room, and sat down under an old floor lamp with a shade decorated with tassels. I often played with these tassels when I was upset, but I was too upset now even to have the strength to touch one. In fact I felt then I was going to die. I felt again somehow like I had the day I and my buddies was all exploded together and we rose into the air like birds, and then fell to the erupting earth and the flames and the screams of aircraft and sirens and men calling through punctured bowels and brains. My face was bathed in a film like tears, but it wasn't tears, it was the sweat of death.

My back was to the kitchen, you see, so I hardly noticed this hand on the back of my neck. It was a warm soft hand not unlike the goat. It moved gently on the nape of my neck, and then after it seemed I had gone to sleep I heard his sort of hillbilly, sort of goat voice inquiring, "*You was talking about an applicant.*"

"What of it?" I cried, taking hold of his hand and throwing it off of me like you would a beetle that had crawled on you.

"Well," he said, putting his hand back on my neck, "I wondered what a applicant did."

36

I wheeled round then and looked at him, for I had decided all of a sudden he was some runaway from the law.

"What would I want with a applicant who pukes when he looks at me, huh?" I shouted at him, beginning to rave. "A fucking little trespasser who feels he must puke and maybe shit when he sees my face. Get out! Get out of my house and off of my property, you little crud."

He only looked at me then with his questioning sky-open eyes.

"What are the duties of this applicant?" he wondered, quiet as a spring zephyr.

My anger simmered down as I studied his eyes, and the vacant space of his missing teeth.

"What does he do?" I repeated after him, as if he had put me under a quieting draught like the doc used to hand me in a little paraffin cup full of something red and drowsy . . . "Why, what does a applicant do?" I said, staring at him like I had just awoke in the hospital and the nurse stood there and said, *"You're better, Garnet."*

"Can you bear messages?" I began cautiously with the most important duty. "That is deliver and fetch letters from down the road?"

"I don't see why not," he contested.

"I reckon you're too good, being white, to rub feet."

"I could take a try at that," he said, looking down at my shoes.

"What size shoe do you wear?" he wondered.

I swallowed hard, and then replied, "Thirteen."

"That's a lot of rubbin'," he remarked, and suddenly we both laughed.

37

He avoided looking at my face still, and I don't suppose anybody ever got any pleasure looking at it, but of course once the girls in school had liked to gaze at me and flirt, that's no exaggeration either, I was once able to put a crush on all the girls, well, that was like an age ago, if not in time, in events . . .

"And is there any payment?" he went on warming up with questions.

"Usually I give only board and room, but well, in your case, I guess . . . spending money is in order."

He nodded.

"Where's my bed?" he queried, looking up at a big stopped grandfather clock.

"Down the hall. But it's in the same room next to mine, you see." I studied him . . . "In case I die in the night, you see," I joked, "I would want you to put some pennies on my eyelids . . ."

He sort of grinned.

"My name, by the way," he offered his hand, "is Daventry."

"And where did you run off from, Daventry?" I inquired, and then put my hand gentle over his mouth and said, "Don't answer that one."

He complained about all the birds making so much noise in the morning he couldn't sleep—oh maybe complain is not the word but *comment.* Then he said he had never seen so many books in a house. There were more books than wallpaper, furniture, pictures, or proper rugs. I told him the books was not mine.

"In the winter"—I went to his first point of criticism—
"the birds for the most part are quiet, oh a few chickadees
scold and call and a crow here and there caws of course.
But until you spoke of it I guess I hadn't any note of the
fuss the birds do make of a morning . . . Now you come
from Utah, Daventry . . . That is plains, isn't it?"

He nodded, as he went from one shelf after another,
taking the books down, blowing off the settled dust, staring at a page here, another page there.

Meanwhile I was holding my breath, trying to work myself up to having him take his first letter to deliver to
Widow Rance. I wondered if he would do, for with all the
"interviewing" of applicants I had done, and with none of
them panning out, if this one didn't work, I would have
to fall back on Quintus, for I couldn't go on seeing all
these young men forever, picking and choosing and being
disappointed. But speaking of Quintus, as I sat there in a
study, I suddenly thought of the word for him, he was
sober, maybe not too sober, but sober. I don't mean in re-
gard to not drinking, I don't dare drink myself, on account
of my veins and arteries being all but murdered, but
Quintus when you got right down to it, didn't approve of
anything but doing chores for his ma and watching the
chickens grow up. Too perfect, Quintus—he made me feel
no-account. Still, if this Daventry doesn't pan, I thought,
I will have to have Quintus forever on account of I can't
keep on interviewing the whole world.

"Oh, Christ Jesus," I let slip out, and he said immediately, "What's wrong with you now?"

"Nothing. Can't I sigh if I want to?"

He began looking at me from that moment more and more straight in the face without so much as batting an eye.

"How did you sleep last night, Daventry?"

"Oh I slept good."

"I don't snore or anything do I?"

"Didn't hear you."

I was looking through an old book on Arabia, trying to get my inspiration up to pen or rather dictate a letter to Daventry for the Widow Rance—my own hands will barely hold a pen anyhow, and for some time now if they hold anything too long all the flesh will come off clear to the bone . . .

"Are you ready, Daventry?" I spoke in my most quavering voice, and I jumped up from my chair and went and stood in the middle of the room ready to dictate and I always felt like the leading baritone in the church choir when I done that, but instead of music of course it was just letters that came out, and this leads me to a remark he made right at the first and shows how he was, for I had begun the letter like this, *My precious Dear, I am sending you a courtly young man named Daventry.*

I will not say he was angered by this sentence, but I could see he had been troubled by something about me from the start, not my nauseous appearance (though as I want to never fail to emphasize, at night or in dim house-light I am still not a million miles away from what I was when the high school girls mooned over me), but by what I spoke.

So there he was the new applicant making a little speech, which begun something like this, "*Where do you get all those odd expressions, Garnet,*" he began talking to me as familiar as if he had knowed me all my days, "*for I never have heard anybody talk like you, and I don't think anybody does talk like you.*"

"*Like the word courtly young man,*" he swept right along.

He stood there now like a judge behind a bench awaiting for my defense.

"As I was saying, Daventry," I began in the greatest confusion at his charge, "not knowing I talked any different from anybody, when we talked earlier, not seeing many persons but the applicants and people not liking to talk to me since I was blowed up for dead, and my buddies all killed and parts of their bodies blown over me, buried under them for some days you know before I was found (I go off on this speech every so often when I know I should follow Doc's advice and forget), you know, well of course in the beginning I spoke like all Virginia boys do, and that is a good speech, but when I fell in love all over again with the Widow Rance and had nothing anyhow to do but read these books, which I will be the first to say I don't understand a jot or tittle of, but all the same I have become habituated to reading these hard tomes I can't understand: for instance I don't take any pleasure anymore in reading the newspapers, and anyhow they are about the living, Daventry, and writ in living language, no, I have got firmly habituated to these old books, like this thick one here about Arabia nearly two hundred years ago, and so gradually you see these old books have seeped or trickled into my speech and have took over maybe from the way people talk today. But until you spoke just now I didn't know I had this peculiarity even. So that explains how I call you a courtly young man, dig?"

Daventry shook his head slowly again like the old half-broken pendulum of the clock when I am dickering with it.

"So I talk now the way it gives me pleasure," I went on somewhat offended at his criticism. "If you don't understand anything I say," I appealed to his forbearance, "ask me, and I will try to explain it then, although the Sunday School superintendent when he was up here a year or so back said I didn't know how to use any of the words right I do pick up from the old tomes, though he was half-joking, and you are serious . . . Well, back to the Widow Rance . . ."

"Just one second, though, Garnet," he began again, "if you don't mind . . . What do I do now if, say, the Widow Rance, as you call her" (I could see he felt this way of speaking of her was queer) . . . "what if she don't want me to deliver these letters, I mean you said something kind of suspicious about her maybe not wanting you to write them."

"To tell the truth," I took up his point, "she don't want my letters." I got somewhat sheepish now. "But the preacher," my voice got persuasive, "talked to her about it, and well, hell, to tell you the truth it's charity . . ."

"Charity?"

"Yes, God damn it!" And in the old days I would have

42

flushed a angry beet-red at having to eat humble pie like this in front of another man, and admit to groveling, but being so discolored I don't suppose if I did flush it would be visible, for instance I can't bear to study myself in the mirror unless all the lights is out except for a teeny candle, then in the darkness and teeny illumination I sometimes look at myself in a bowl of water, and is what I see sad, well . . .

"Don't be downhearted," I returned to Daventry. "She will receive you, if not with open arms, as a respected messenger, if not a guest."

Again he shook his head, but he had the freshly sharpened pencil ready, and was ready to go:

Dearest, only dear, I began all over again,

> I am getting on better now, and some adjustments are being made. I have goats now, which are mine from the death of Mr. Pettison, brought by Quintus, who by the way I thought of as having as an applicant, and I believe he will look in on me from time to time, but, dear lady, this letter is to introduce you to . . . Daventry . . . He is from the grazing lands of Utah, and will be attending me as an applicant. I believe him and me will get on, and I would like to have you trust him also. Never fear, I will never ever again intrude myself on your presence, and remember there is nothing on or about my person which can bring disease or other complications because the army docs assured me without quite swearing on the Bible I am absolutely sterilized from any Indo China germs, so

be of good cheer. And know that I love you more
than life.

Your servant,   Garnet

I had not been studying his face whilst I was dictating
because the effort and pain of expressing my thoughts had
taken all my attention and strength, but when I looked
down on him from my six feet four I was struck with
amazement at his expression. He was looking at me with a
kind of sick awe, certainly with amazed wonder.

"What is it?" Daventry, I inquired.

"Nothing, Garnet."

"Yes, there is something. You think I'm crazy, don't
you . . . ?"

"No I don't," Daventry countered. "I don't think that."

"Well . . ."

"I just wonder at it all," he spoke after a while in a
whisper. Then all of a sudden he swatted a daytime mos-
quito that had settled on his cheek, and having swatted it
his cheek was all covered with blood for it must have been
biting us all night. I walked over to him, and almost without thinking I was going to do it, took out a clean pocket
handkerchief and wiped the blood from off his face. He
looked at me with more wonder.

"Now, Daventry," I went on, "we seal this letter just as
though it was to go through the U.S. mails, and you walk
the mile and a half or so down the back road and put it in
her hands."

"With pleasure," he said, jumping up like he was coming

to from a nap, and took the letter from my loose hands.

When he was gone, I put my face to the wall and began to bawl.

"He pities me, God damn it," I said, *"that's what that look meant, and God damn it and him I won't have it. I won't have the motherfucker pity me . . ."*

And at the same time I was celestially happy at the look he had given me.

It was the first time for I don't know when that someone had looked at me like I was another man, a little nauseated sure, but still like he seen me as I was. And here I was too almost shedding tears for the first time in so long after writing down on these slips of paper that I could not cry, well, it was mostly bawling, not real tears come out from my lachrymal glands, but still some did. A milestone.

———————

When he was gone, then, when nobody was about and the shadows begin to fall, my own secret from everybody would come to the fore. Everybody knows about my secret of reading books I don't properly understand, whose words I don't properly fathom, but I don't think anybody had found out where I go when all is dark and still. I left Virginia when I was only, as folks reminded me, little more than a boy, seventeen, and went to war, but though I was gone some nine years, I did not come back so much a man, which is what the sergeant and the captain promised us when we had took the oath of allegiance, I came back like somebody immemorial, drained of everything except some tiny shreds of memory. For I felt I had been gone a million years. Not only did I come back looking like somebody that was not me, but everybody close to me had left or died, the old houses were vacant about the seashore, and the young men and women were either gone or looked old and unremembering. I mentioned I believe some time ago that I was this great dancer, loved to dance all night, danced in the ballroom long after the band had left if any young girl would stay on. Then we would go out beside the side entrance of the hall, where the musicians used to come in carrying their instruments, beside a little dam over the old river, and neck and spoon and kiss until dawn. Then we would walk home hand in hand as slow as clouds when there is no breeze.

That dance hall has long been in disuse, partly because of the long war I was in, and young people have left for all other parts of the country, and the people who are left don't dance. There is a shortcut to this dance hall nobody knows but me, right back of my property, there is a sort of little steep cliff you climb, and once at the top a good fifty feet or so you go for quite a stretch through little pine trees, and rough ground, then you come to a pond that shines most blue at night, and beyond the pond is another incline, then more trees, and from the top of a sort of cliff again you look down on the Marigold Meadows, though the sign with these big letters is defaced, certainly the light-bulbs that illuminated the letters are nearly all gone, the

big windows are all busted, the great staircase which led
to the box office is full of rubble and pine cones so that you
have to take a running jump and leap over it, but once inside things look somewhat the same, the big dance floor itself almost the size of an acre is still sort of shiny like just
polished, the bandstand is still up where some of the best
saxophonists and piano players once sat, and above the floor
itself is that great revolving many-colored moon which
flicked down on us dancers all its purple and red and
orange and white motes, turning us into strange creatures
who were I do swear experiencing our only happiness. The
many-colored moon above us turned us into people with
entirely different clothes from what we had on, our hair
became purple, our hands orange, our shoes diamond
studded, but the happiness in our eyes was our own as we
pressed against our young girls' nipples and firm belly, we
lost all track of time or where we had driven in from, or
our names or tomorrow, yes, for those few hours in the
Marigold Meadows it was, who knows? . . . almost worth
having been born, we could say anyhow we were full of
some sort of pure joy.

I would return there secretly, then, when night came,
would light a candle which I kept there, for I feared the
law might see any stronger illumination and come to in-
vestigate, a phonograph, a windup kind, had been left behind with some old records, some jazz, a few rock, and I
would turn it on and dance with myself, the candle making
the many-colored moon seem to gyrate again until one
visit very late I found by turning a switch the damned

thing did work just like in past times. But mostly I sat at the piano, which though missing a few black keys could still be played, and I would strum a little, and then before I knew it it was dawn.

When Daventry moved in I felt I would not dare go so often, and would have to wait also until he was asleep and then I would steal out. The first night I did it I don't think he noticed, but after that, well, I am getting ahead of my story, and what I am trying to recollect now is how he had gone to the Widow Rance with my latest letter, and I was sitting on pins and needles wondering how she was going to take the new applicant.

"You was gone one whale of a time" was what I had decided to say to him when he got back, but somehow when he did walk in, I felt too glad to see him to scold him. What I had feared all the time he was away, without quite knowing it then, was that he had left me. So, I would have looked pale with worry when he sort of tiptoed in late had my complexion not been transformed by war not to show pallor.

He looked at me for some time. I didn't know what that look meant, and as a matter of fact I was thinking too how I was going to sneak off to the dance hall without being missed. You see, it had to be kept secret. I didn't want him or nobody to know I went there. It was all that was left of my past life, when I had been young and personable, the blood had coursed in my veins, everything was ahead, everything was *then* and *now*, there was no yesterday or tomorrow, and now there is no time at all, tomorrow is not a word I can pronounce, there is no *now* really, and yesterday I never think of except as dance music. All I have is the letters, the applicants, and the dance hall, and none of them is real. I do not even believe in death because what I am is emptier than death itself.

"So how did you find the Widow Rance?" I said in my tough soldier voice, which some people have described as coming from my big size thirteen shoes.

He sat down, and looked nowhere now in particular.

"She accepted the letter," he began, "but then she made me read it to her." He passed his hand over his face, and a strand of his corn-tassel hair came down.

"That's new," I informed him. "Of course, the other bearers was mostly black fellows, so maybe your color has something to do with it."

I ushered him now to come with me into the parlor, where we hardly ever went because it is the most stiff and grandfathery of all the rooms.

"Where did she have you sit?" I wondered after we got settled.

"We went into a parlor like this one," Daventry replied, looking around this unfamiliar part of the house. "She offered me some shortbread and coffee."

He stood up then, sort of bending like a young choke-cherry tree in one of our bad winds. "Then, Garnet," he went on, "as I said she made me read the letter to her, but instead of reading it once or even twice, I had to read it a dozen times . . ."

"And you obliged her . . . a dozen?" I sort of gasped. It

was me now that was not looking at him, and he was looking at me full in the face like I was any other fellow he had ever met.

"She is a beautiful young woman."

Later I realized he had said this sentence in a prayerful way.

"The way I came upon her," I began, like when I talk to myself, *"is like this. I was walking in the woods shortly after I come back from over there you know."* I stopped just a second on that word *there*. *"I had been back only a short time, and everything looked different. I mean I could find my way around but it was like I was using a map of a place I had never yet visited, for the real terrain didn't seem like mine or where I was born. But I knew of course her house, it is one of the biggest and whitest in this part of the state. It was night on this time of my return home, and I stopped in a clump of woods, and without warning see her in her kitchen. She had no lights on but a kerosene lamp. I knew her at once after all the years, and I was about to turn back into the clump of woods and go the short stretch home, when all of a sudden she took off her blouse, and began to work up some kind of ointment there in the palm of one hand, which later I was to learn was cocoa butter, and she began to massage her nipples with this butter, oh so gently so tenderly, and I became so excited. I was like somebody who had eat of some strange plant, I had to hold my own mouth shut with my handkerchief, I bit my lips not to cry out and terrify her. I was so aroused, Daventry, so beside myself, I fell to the base of an old pine*

tree. *I came then all over myself like I had burst open all my insides through and through, I felt like all my manhood had gushed out of me. She turned out the light by and by and I lay at the base of the tree on a carpet of pine needles. I don't know if I had passed out or not. I lay on them pine needles carpet till morning . . ."*

There began to be a division of work in my household largely owing to the fact that Daventry didn't have all his front teeth and when he read to me this imperfection of his made me not understand all the words and his tongue moving across the upper part of his mouth like a snake's also got a bit on my nerves but only when he read.

But just before the division was made and Quintus appointed as reader, I think Daventry suspected me, I mean suspected about me going to the dance hall. I mean I think he knew I had a secret. I didn't know yet about his secret. But then he was all secrets. He should have been called Secret Daventry instead of Potter Daventry. Yes, his Christian name he kept a secret too for some weeks, and can you blame him, for Potter is about the worst name I ever heard baptized on a boy, if Daventry ever was baptized.

Quintus then was reinstated for reading, and he was sitting in a big straw-bottomed chair with dime-store glasses on, reading to me out of one of the more ancient of the books I have inherited:

"Before the victory of Lucius Lucullus in the war
against Mithridates, that is down to 74 B.C., there were
no cherry tress in Italy. Lucullus first imported them
from Pontus . . ."

"Where you going, Daventry?" I interrupted the reading, or rather just punctuated it, for Quintus went right on:

". . . and in 120 years they have crossed the ocean and
got as far as Britain."

"Why, the Widow Rance asked me to stop by her place
this evening," he replied to my question.

"But all the same no attention has succeeded in getting
cherries to grow in Egypt. Of cherries the Arponian
are the reddest, and the Lutatian the blackest, while
the Caecilian kind is . . ."

"All right, Quints," I said, "that will do for the P.M."
I walked over to where Daventry was sort of slouching
by the kitchen screen door, his hand in midair about to
reach for the latch.

"You know I haven't had time to write her a message today," I told him.

"I know that," he replied, sort of uppity I thought. I
swallowed hard.

The understanding was you go only when you bear
messages were the words that were about to come forth,
but I checked them, and said instead. "Supposing you sit
down a while until I pen a short message for you to take
her." I tried to keep the anger out of my voice.

"Suit yourself," he mumbled.

I knew then he had been invited back by the Widow. My head was swimming, yet I had to go through with the pretense of writing her something. No words at all would come to me, except the usual old salutation *My Only Darling* when here she was driven to retch when she only thought of me, and yet, wait a moment now, I had been told nonetheless by two different parties she kept my letters, so at least the letters was all right and that gave me the second wind to give out.

> I have split up the household chores now between Quintus and Daventry, and soon we are going to give a big party here when everything is painted and the Congoleum rugs brought down from the attic. We are also going to grow plants indoors so that in the winter it will look gay here. I am sure you found Daventry the most . . .

The pen had froze in my hands, for I became aware Daventry himself was standing over me watching my hand. The effrontery, the nerve, the cool gall. But instead of taking my ire out on Daventry it was poor Quintus now I rated and abused, for I could hear his honey voice still reading from that old Roman history book, like an elocution pupil, droning on about a Roman cherry which has an agreeable flavor but only if it is eaten under the tree on which it grows as it is so delicate that it won't stand carriage.

"Stop it! Stop that!" I found myself shouting so close to

Quintus' glasses that they fogged over, but that devil went right on with his reading aloud.

I licked the envelope, handed the letter to Daventry, and rushed fleeing from my own house into the meadow and then begun to climb the cliff, but of course I could not go to the ruined dance hall now because the sun had not quite sunk out of sight in the western hills.

I sat down then under a little scrub pine, and waited for old Sol to sink like an immense egg yolk into the black skillet of clouds.

Then I heard the pine needles move and Quintus was kneeling down by me, his book in his hand, and went on reading to me. I was too stunned by this mutiny on the part of both my hired men to say a word but sort of eavesdropped you might say on what he was reading, and the thought that neither he nor I really understood what the book was saying sort of struck me funny, though that was the whole point of choosing this kind of book. I required reading that would not make too much sense and would keep down the terrible pain that rises up from my lower guts and is followed by dizziness and lightheadedness, but I think Quintus loved to read things which didn't have any meaning or relevance to him either, but anyhow he read a sentence that late afternoon that kind of left a lasting impression on me, if not him:

> "It is a remarkable fact that the three chief natural elements, water, air, and fire, have neither taste, smell nor any flavor whatsoever."

"Read that once again, Quints," I commanded him. But Quintus went right on with the next sentence, informing me,

"In the meantime we find that there are ten kinds of flavors, sweet, luscious, unctuous, bitter, rough, acrid, sharp, harsh, acid and salt.

"My day's work is up!" Quintus said, looking at an old pocket watch.

"Do you know something, Quints?" I began. "I think Daventry is . . . is . . . is . . ."

Quintus took off his store glasses and blinked at me.

"What do you think, Quintus?" I said finally, looking off into the now dark west.

"I think you think," he began in a kind of sassing way, "I think you think they sweet on one another without they having had any time yet for even getting acquainted."

And then gazing at me with his big almond-shaped eyes, he began nodding again and again at me until at last irritated with this repeated movement I took hold of his head in both my hands and held it quiet like I was stopping the pendulum of a clock.

I don't know what time Daventry came home that night, I had drifted out to dreamland, I was dreaming about a black woman who had come in to make me a pan of rice, and she was having trouble getting little brown specks out of it which she said had to be removed before she could serve it to me.

Then gradually out of this dream I felt the warmth of a human presence next to me, and not opening my eyes for fear—well, yes, just for fear—I gradually moved my fingers, which by the way had burst open again owing to my injuries, revealing, if one cared to look, the bones, anyhow my fingers moved over and found a hand on my coverlet, and the hand closed over my fingers. I did not need to open my eyes to know it was Daventry.

"There is something troubling me," he began, "and I got to confide to somebody. Will you hear me out?"

"You've made love to the Widow Rance, haven't you?" I whispered, but for some reason I let him go on holding my hand, though his powerful grip hurt the flesh.

"Oh, are you raving. That ain't what is on my mind, Garnet, at all."

"But I can tell by the way you paused there is something between you two."

"Well, she did kiss me good night." His voice was sultry and distempered as he got this out.

"You see," I cried, throwing off his grasp, but he took my hand again in his and held it.

"I can't ever love again, Garnet," he started up again. "So be easy. I got to get this confession off my chest meanwhile."

"You don't love the Widow Rance?"

"No, of course not. How could I love anybody after what I done, and after what may happen to me?"

"Why don't you love her when she is so luscious beautiful?" I wondered, working myself up.

"Listen here, Garnet. When I was in Utah, I had this terrible fight with two men come up to me one night behind the Ebenezer Baptist Church, which adjoins my father's sheep ranch. They jumped me, Garnet, with knives. I think they mistook me for somebody else. They didn't want my money. They simply said, '*The world isn't big enough for us with you in it . . .*' Garnet, are you listening to me?"

"Just tell me outright you didn't have the Widow Rance tonight." I leaned up on one elbow.

"Oh, Garnet, God Awmighty, how could I love anybody when I've got this heavy burden?"

"Did you lose your teeth in this fight?" I questioned on.

He nodded or maybe he shook his head, though it was so dark it was more by the way the air moved as he whirled his long head of hair than by my seeing him do so.

"Well, then, what happened behind this church?" I pursued the subject dispiritedly.

"I killed both of them, Garnet. But I didn't know I had it in me to kill. I killed them so *thorough*, don't you see? Like a executioner, trained and true."

"But if it was your life or theirs, Daventry . . ."

He had laid his head now down over my chest, and went on like this. "Maybe," he began again, "I was brought up too religious, I don't know, yes of course you're right I killed

57

in self-defense, didn't I? But when I laid them out there on the ground killed with their own knives—I stood a long time over their bodies, and I will never get over it, not if I live to . . ."

"If you're that religious will you swear on the Holy Bible you did not enjoy her body tonight, Daventry?"

He shook so with sobs then and he was laying across me like I was his last refuge that for a minute I did not realize what was happening. For the first time since I had been ruined and stained like mulberry wine, another human being had forgot how horrible I am, and was touching me and hugging me and asking for comfort, forgetting how I look like some abortion or night-goblin, though as I told you before, in the dark somehow I am sort of good-looking again.

I raised him up and got out of bed to get the Bible, and when I came back I lit the lamp, and held the book open for him. Even when the lamp came on, though, he did not seem to see me as nauseous this time, he put his hand on the book and swore he had not touched the body of the Widow Rance. I did not ask him if he would later.

He slept sort of on my chest all night, but waking every now and again to tell me he could not bear the weight of having killed these two young men.

"Well, what about me?" I finally cried, and raised his head up and looked at him in the eyes.

"Well," he whimpered, waiting.

"I have killed over a hundred."

"I see," he sobbed. "But they're not coming after you

for it, on account of you was sent to do it in line with your duty as a soldier."

"They're not coming after you either," I said firmly. I put my hand in his hair, and it was sopping wet with sweat. His tears also had wet my nightshirt through and through.

"God will come for me though," he said at last, and those words froze my spine. My jaw trembled, and I felt cold all over.

I smoothed his hair, and finally, well, since he was the only one who had dared touch me, for the doc had done it oh so gingerly, for it was like touching the insides of a man, so that the doc had said once (I guess more in pity than revulsion), *"Well, Garnet, you look like an open anatomy chart, one can see all your veins and arteries moving with their blood."*

"Daventry," I began after a long silence, and the words I spoke coming in fact as a considerable surprise to myself, "if the Widow wants you, you can let her have you . . . I won't be jealous."

"I couldn't. I couldn't. You know that I can't."

"Yes, you can," I comforted him. "You are my only friend. Maybe God sent you to me . . . Daventry, you killed in self-defense, and that was way back in Utah. What sort of men was they, by the way?"

"Mexicans."

"Well, then," I said, "you forget it."

"God will send his messenger." Daventry was firm. "You'll see."

"Then what about me?" I moved so that his chest came off my arms.

"Ain't you suffered enough?" He began to look at me, and suddenly I think he saw me again as he had the first day when he had wanted to throw up at the sight of me, but now I was the sharer of his secret and so he held me tight again, as though a little child at last had embraced the dark goblin that has hid so long by the foot of his bed.

We didn't sleep a wink that night, but his crying and scalding tears made my own dried-up lachrymal glands feel a bit easier. We were held then in bond to one another. Even Quintus noticed the next morning. Why do I say *even*. He sees through everything.

Quintus had taken to reciting now from old books of poetry, which I don't think either of us enjoyed, but sometimes a verse here and there of what he recited would stick in my mind more than the books that was in prose, and there was some verses he read one day which kept running about in my mind forever after:

> Lilac River, as you go to sea,
> bear you any news
> of her you took from me?

I wondered what those words meant, I mean meant to me to the point that they arrested me so and would not leave my mind, or rather my mouth and tongue, they were always there, and then another thing Quintus said that same day after the poem which struck me almost more forcibly:

At noon you don't have no shadow;
it's then the Devil has power over you.

Almost like somebody who is trying to gain time when he is in a tight spot I changed the subject because the verses and the warning so disturbed me, and said, "Quintus, you are getting smitten on those old books almost more than me . . . Maybe you should take a correspondence course in high school."

"I already been through high school," came his icy reply.

"Well, then college, Quints."

"Aha," he said in his snottiest way, but I was not thinking about his high-school or college career really and truly then, but about that idea of his which was pure nigger superstition I suppose about my having no shadow right then on account of it was high noon. That is how my mind works now, I am always troubled about something I thought a few minutes ago so that I don't always hear what people say to me at this moment now, for my thoughts anyhow are far away, and so all of a sudden I said to Quintus, "That *her* in the Lilac River poem is Georgina" (which was the first name of the Widow Rance).

"Oh no it ain't," Quintus replied. "It's nobody."

"It's anybody who hears it wants it to be."

He studied me for a long uneasy time, and then he said, "*You're getting awful cosy with the runaway.*"

"Oh. Well, you didn't like taking and fetching messages, that's for sure."

"Never denied you, did I?" Quintus shot back.

He got so now he read on and on in the books to himself, and didn't always share with me aloud. Anyhow he knew at noon now I was most sleepy (together with the fact that I didn't have no shadow) owing to the fact the runaway, as he called him, kept me up all night.

I woke up a little later in the P.M. however long enough, my head against a young poplar tree, to hear Quintus' honey voice going it again:

> "With one son dead at his side, and another shot through, he felt the pulse of his dying son with one hand and held his rifle with the other, and commanded the men to sell their lives as dearly as they could. Yet the remorseless spirit which governed the stern Puritan that terrible night on the Pottawatomie had departed . . ."

"Who you reading about now, Quintus?" I queried, noticing too just like he had said there was damned few shadows about still.

"Why, John Brown," he answered right back.

"Well, if you ain't turning into a God-damned Yankee now before my eyes."

"*You should beware of Daventry.*" Quintus spoke in a

hollow whisper, leaning over me to say this with his glasses still on, and the book laid down on some pine needles.

"It's too late to beware of anybody," I told him . . .

Then looking at him so close to me, I said, "There's an eyewinker loose in the corner of your left eye, and it's going to get into your pupil and blind you if you ain't careful . . . Here, let me take it out before it gets into the inside of your eye."

I removed the eyewinker.

"Don't read anymore today, Quints. I'm already so full of ideas you have give me from all those damned tomes from my grandfather's bookshelves. Jesus Christ, readin' to me about John Brown though is the limit . . . I say, Quintus . . ."

That was the same P.M. Mrs. Gondess from the King William Savings and Loan Association appeared and had herself announced by Daventry before she billowed into the sitting room. Quintus was rubbing my feet because I had begun to have a spell, and there Mrs. Gondess stood before us in a white expensive hand-sewn dress, with a big brooch, and a long string of blue beads and smelling of face powder for ten miles.

"Have a seat, ma'am," I said, disentangling myself from Quintus and stepping over him at last, while he quickly moved away into the next room where he began reading.

Mrs. Gondess stood looking from room to room, but with her gaze more or less focused on the ceiling of each room her eyes visited. Then smiling sadly but still not seeing me, she said, "I won't stay, Garnet," and then her whole head and gaze were lowered like at evening prayer.

She talked about the crops and the weather while avoiding as her main occupation looking at me direct, but of course she had to steal a few peeks at me on account of the human eye always manages to see even more than it may want to.

"The land taxes, Garnet," she said at last, and you would have thought she had mentioned the gayest subject in all of time.

"What about them, Mrs. Gondess?"

"Have you not received the notices?" she cried, her gaiety approaching laughter . . . "We've informed you, Garnet . . . You're in arrears, payment after payment after payment in arrears . . ."

I waited but was really watching Daventry, who stood waiting some distance from us speakers and reminded me of a church usher waiting to get his cue to pass the collection plate.

"I can't believe," she went on, but her gaiety had gone, and her mouth had frozen, "I find it, that is, implausible that you have not received our notices."

And then in the kind of voice one of Quintus' books describe as *ringing*, but was closer to screeching, or come to think of it croaking, she deafened us with "*You have got to pay those taxes or be thrown off your land!*"

I picked up a toothpick I had laid down on a little hand-painted saucer and touched my two front teeth with it, and then put it down.

"I'd think the God-damned Army would pay them for me," I said after a minute.

"No, no, no!" She began in earnest now whether because of the profanity or fear more would come or because she was ready to spout. "I called you on the phone about it last February," she reminded me . . . "Garnet, Garnet, you don't want to lose this fine property over some little back taxes. Just think how far back it goes in your family. Why truth to tell, you are one of the oldest Virginians . . ."

We both stopped our wrangling because we could hear Quintus reading aloud to himself. At first I had thought it was birds. Quintus' out-loud reading had embarrassed Mrs. Gondess, or made her feel awkward or something, and it sort of threw a monkey wrench into what we were talking about, so that there was a long, I mean a preposterous, pause and silence, during which Daventry now finally entered the room in earnest and sat down near the banker.

"You're not going to throw a man who gave his life for his country off his own land and into the road?" Daventry started in.

"I don't believe I've had the pleasure." She turned to me for an explanation of this speech from my applicant.

"Mr. Potter Daventry," I introduced him.

She said "*How do you do*" very quickly and then turned her full attention to him, her back turned toward me now like a slammed door.

"Of course Garnet won't be dispossessed, but he has to pay these back taxes, or he may . . . It's gone to the courts, you see. I can't begin to tell you how serious . . ."

There was more and more, but all I could do and all I remember is how much I admired Daventry, I don't know why, I mean he had a stern beauty as he kind of made her quail before him, and almost promise to stop dispossession.

Finally though she was gone and away in a big shined Cadillac chauffeured by some snooty colored guy with a garrison cap. But her visit cast a pall over all of us.

"So that's all I been waiting for," I began, "I mean I think it is the one thing I lacked, getting dispossessed, as the old girl names it . . . And you, Quintus, would have to read aloud at a time like that, God damn it . . . Don't you think she sees we're a outlandish enough bunch as it is without you mumbling and jawing and mooning aloud over there all by yourself with a book, Jesus Christ!"

"That's right," Quintus countered, "go ahead and blame me for you not payin' your taxes too, and get turned out in the road. Go on, go ahead. Blame me. When you know God-damned well she come here to fight with you, no matter what I done . . . I was engaged here to read and read I will, so don't pull no stuff on me. I've been readin' and I will read till I get good and ready to quit readin' . . ."

Quintus went out slamming the back door, but not very hard, and I watched him go sauntering down toward the cliffs.

I went back into the sitting room and began to walk, sort of veering in the direction of the spinet desk, and sitting down there took out a sheet of very old scented vellum paper.

I felt Daventry's breath on my face as he stole up to say, "I don't want to be the bearer of any more messages to the Widow."

I wheeled around. "You'll do as you're told, or you'll get

out! You shall bear messages for me, do you hear? . . . I have given an order. Your duties are known . . ."

His mouth, which I now saw was beautifully formed (my attention to it had been distracted before by the absence of teeth in the upper jaw), trembled, and his blue eyes looked like they were smarting.

"All right, Garnet, I suppose if you say so . . ."

"I do say so. Dismissed."

But when I turned my attention back to the scented sheet of stationery I couldn't think of anything to say, and kept writing the same salutation again and again.

My Dearest Girl
My Dearest Girl

Since I could not think of anything to write to Georgina, and since I was too mad at Quintus for reading out loud when Mrs. Gondess had been paying her call to summon him for a reading, I began to leaf through a book on phrenology which he had left face down on the big Turkey carpet. Without quite realizing it at the time I was the most upset I had been since I returned to the "land of the living." I felt I would lose my own land and house. There was more to what old lady Gondess said than her polite little warnings delivered while her sheeny Cadillac waited outside with its motor running.

I had to smile at my plight at the same time, for whereas all my other buddies had turned to grass when they were blue, discouraged or pissed-off, here I who should be lying in the same grave with them, go and pick up when in dejection some old book I can't understand and read from it or have read from it until my nerves quiet down.

In this state of mind then I picked up the *Guide to Phrenology*, which was dogeared and with its spine broken and its pages badly foxed, and began the chapter

MAN AS A GLYPH

Man is little more than a glyph which punctuates space, but once gone is as unrecollectable as smoke or clouds.

There kneeling before me as I looked up from this sentence was Daventry. His hair was uncombed and hung almost down to his shoulders, and his mouth was trembling violently.

"Think over your decision, Garnet. Do not send me . . ."

"I'll send you to hell, I will," I cried, mad still that I did not have anything to write in the letter.

"What are you here for," I exclaimed, my voice rising to a wail, "but to deliver and fetch messages, huh? Answer me that one."

"You mean to treat me then like a slave in bondage because of my sharing my secret with you?"

"You can earn your keep the same as Quintus. What's so wonderful special about you that you can't hoof two miles down the road to see the Widow or Georgina, as you called her the other day, with your new cosihood?"

"You see, Garnet, you're egging me on with her, and then you'll turn on me!"

"Turn, hell," I said, somewhat peaceable again. "I've got a lot on my mind, that's all. Matter of fact, too, I've run out of things to write to her. I've told her all I know, and she ain't told me so much as a sigh of breath in return."

Daventry was rubbing my feet, as I guess he feared I was about to have an attack, though actually it was only Quintus who was supposed to do this service for me.

"Supposing I write the letter for you then," Daventry said, taking a rest from his rubbing.

"Yeah, supposin' . . . Do you know how to write good letters?"

He nodded vigorously.

"Well, why in cruddy hell didn't you tell me earlier? Are you, do you mean to tell me, an educated man?"

"I did go through college," he admitted.

"Another of your well-kept secrets, huh? . . . And look here, I don't believe that shit about you killing two men."

"Suit yourself, Garnet."

"By the by, do you know what a *glyph* is?" I sort of cooled off a bit and begun studying the paragraph in the phrenology book.

"No, but I can find out for you." He was all cooperation and eagerness. And after a slight pause, rubbing my feet some more, he said, *"Don't send me, Garnet, please please don't."*

"You have found favor in her eyes," I half-quoted something to him in a whisper.

He shook his head, his eyes were full of salt tears.

"Supposing," I said, standing up, "supposing, Daventry,

69

you dictate the letter, and I will write it down this time."
I let him bawl for a while, and watching him cry was the
beginning of maybe the second terrible thing that had happened to me in recent days. As I watched him so helpless,
so downcast and downhearted, so lonely and without people, and despite his lie about being through college, so
young and actually very good-looking, I had a strange glow
of tenderness like I had never had for any other person before, not even my buddies who was blown to bits before
my open eyes.

"A *glyph*," he said, through his choking grief, "a glyph,
Garnet, must mean judging by the context of the sentence
you have your finger on, a sign standing for something
else."

"That's clear as mud." I slammed the book shut.

I went over to an old card table, and took up a stenog-
rapher's pad, and a sharp pencil. "All right, Daventry," I
said, "shoot!"

He mooned a while longer, not even bothering to wipe
his face dry of his tears, he just let them dry on him like a
three-year-old.

My Only Darling,

he began,

When I told you the last time you were all I had
you did not believe me. Believe me now, dearest. Without you, without the knowledge you are there beyond
the maple grove, in your beautiful white-pillared house,

70

my days would be without sunshine or hope. I do not expect you to return my love, I owe you my life if you will let me tell you how I adore you. By granting me this favor, you will have granted me all. Do not detain my messenger, dear girl, but read the message, if you like, in his presence, and then dismiss him. Yours, for all time, ever,

Garnet Montrose

As I formed the last letter of my name, we both exchanged what was like one single same terrible look, a look like two shots which met and exploded together in the air.

———————————

I knew as I watched Daventry go with the message he himself had composed that it was going to happen, but I didn't know the full terrible effect it was to have on me. I mean I thought I could die, was going to die pretty shortly, but I didn't know there was so much pain left in my body that should already be dead. But when Quintus heard him leave, I think he knowed it, for he came into my bedroom, where I was already like laid out, and looked at me hard.

"I don't want to be read to, Quints," I said.

"Do you want your nightshirt put on?" he said.

"It ain't late enough to go to sleep," I pointed out.

"Well, you're in bed though."

"All right, put me in my nightshirt, why don't you?"

He had a terrible time getting me into it, for all of a

sudden all the strength and power had gone out of my body, like it had when they first brought me into that army hospital and even the nurses and orderlies let out little moans and oh's.

"Your white master ain't feelin so good today, Quints," I mumbled when he got me in between the sheets.

"Should I call the doc?"

I just shook my head a good many times because the motion kept me from feeling so dizzy.

Quintus began rubbing my feet, I think in pure desperation, and all at once I said a thing that made me as sick as if I had heard it on the news broadcast: *He will fuck her tonight.*

"Oh no he won't, Garnet," Quintus answered back. "She's too upper for him."

"Don't you spoil me now." I tried to raise my voice, and laughed.

It got fearful hot that night, well, we was about in July if I remember this review of my life, I think I saw a few fireflies floating around which means it was getting later into the summer.

That was the time Quints and me became almost as close as Daventry and me was getting before he stepped into the trap I had laid for him—to use his way of explaining it all.

"I ain't going to die, Quints, so you don't need to sit up."

Well, he was already asleep in that mammoth old stuffed chair. He slept good and snored as loud as a water buffalo, but when the pains came I would hold his hand tight but he never woke up.

You see, I would talk to myself, telling myself the same story I have already told so many times, but it helped explain things somehow when I got in this state, when I was blown up, all my veins and arteries moved from the inside where they belong to the outside so that as that army doc put it, I have been turned inside out in all respects.

The hall clock struck three in the morning. Quintus stirred a little. A helpful breeze came drifting in, and brought me Quintus' smell, which was like those night moths that hit you in the chest when you run sometimes through the woods as a boy.

"Quints," I shook him," what do I smell like? You never told me."

"Stale shortbread," he spoke in his sleep.

"Are you awake, Quints?"

"Old socks," he said. He was sound asleep but he heard me too.

When morning came he brought me my coffee, but my tongue was hanging out, and my eyes were losing their focus. Daventry had not showed.

"Can't you drink so much as a swallow?" Quints watched me try to down a sip of his strong brew. If I could have seen him I would have knowed he was scared, petrified, sick almost as me, etc., but my eyes did not focus now at all.

"I'll call Doc then," he mumbled, going off.

I couldn't move then to do a thing.

I don't remember anything till evening, and Doc come in with his old beat-up bag which might have looked black in 1923, but was now just all wrinkles and creases and holes but with still enough leather to hold the medicines and syringe. He took out the needle right away the minute he seen me and I knew I was in for oblivion for maybe a day.

Doc told Quints a lot of things then, I could hear the words but not know the meaning, yet I knew kind of, it was like I had consumed a whole haymow of grass, and then I didn't want to die after all, this life which was not worth the candle—I wanted to keep after all.

"Doc," I began, trying to see in which corner of the room he was sitting, "Doc, can you hold me till Daventry comes, or did the son of a bitch go to Utah?"

I could sort of imagine the questioning look on the doc's face, and the last I heard was Quintus telling him something on the subject of due taxes and dispossession.

It was after dawn, the birds were making a big fuss still, though they make their biggest to-do of course before dawn, but I knew it was after dawn by the way the light was pearl-gray on the cliff out there. So I wasn't in the next world, but I wasn't glad after all to be back, because of the pain.

Quintus was making me drink some bouillon as strong-tasting as the sweat off a horse.

"He's waiting in the next room," Quintus finally announced. "He spent the night in my room."

"How many nights is this he's been gone?" I inquired.

"Well, ah, let me see," Quintus pondered. "Four."

"I been hovering four nights then . . . I'll be God-damned."

Daventry came in. He looked all dolled up, and sheepish, and troubled, but I felt as exhausted as if I had lifted a horse and dray.

"No, I didn't," he said to that look on my face.

"You're a fucking liar."

"But she wanted me to, Garnet."

"And you mean to tell me, you big stiff, you didn't then?"

"I don't think she really wanted it," he went on.

I began to doubt if I was awake or still under the hypo-dermic, but I know now I was awake all right.

"I don't know how to tell you, Garnet," he mumbled on.

"Well, don't wear yourself out in trying."

"She is though in love with me. That's for sure."

"Aha, good. Well, it was your beautiful letter done it, and your general overall appearance."

"All she wanted to do was look at me naked, she said, for the time being."

I raised up on my left elbow at that, but it give out right away and I fell back on the matress.

"I stripped for her, since she wanted that, and she kissed

75

me all over. She nearly drove me mad then, but she wouldn't go beyond the kissing and feeling up . . . I ran out, but I couldn't come home here . . . I stayed in some . . . old deserted crumbling dance hall . . ."

Daventry didn't understand, nor did Quintus, nor did I why I screamed so, I got up and as I did I fell through the open window onto the lawn below. It was a wonder I didn't kill myself, but the concussion made me feel better. They carried me in.

My grief, after I thought about it, was of course that he had discovered my secret. I didn't want anybody to go to my ruined dance hall. Here he had taken my girl away from me in a worse way than if he had fucked her, and now he had stolen my secret.

I was sick then for about a month, and after that I got up and was strong again and decided I would live. But the next day they showed me the foreclosure notice. We was to have to vacate my grandfather's and my great-grand-father's house.

"See here. I will get you the money, Garnet," Daventry told me while rubbing my feet.

While I was studying the foreclosure and dispossession papers which Mrs. Gondess had sent me, and was wondering what I would do with all my furniture, or rather my grandfather's and great-grandfather's furniture, when I should be thrown out on the road, I was eyeing a strange long ancient limousine drawing up in the front driveway that looked like it was from the time of the 'twenties, or out from a museum, and this tall black gent gets out. I thought for a while I had smoked the wrong kind of grass, which by the way Daventry had brought. He said he only took it up after he became a murderer, and I noticed it didn't agree with him too much, so he left it all for me, but since I have these pills that the doc left, I don't use it, and it has all gone to Quintus.

All the same this black man was coming up the road to my house step by step, as slow and self-possessed as if he had taken that walk every day of his life and belonged on my property to boot, and I could hear my breathing getting louder and louder just like it does before I have a spell. Then I heard him ring the front-door bell, which I haven't heard rung for I don't know how long. This trumpet-clarion made the birds all stop singing and must have been carried to any boats at sea. Quintus stood up with a big book in his hand but I motioned him to stand right where he was, and I went to the front door and was about to say "Good evenin'" when the arrival sang out, "Is Quintus Isham within?"

He was lordly and never looked at me once, but kept his eye on the wren house over the arch of the door.

"Quintus Pearch you mean," I amended his question.

"Is he within?"

"Well," I said, disgusted, "why don't you come in and see," and I opened the screen, he hesitated a while, pulling on one of his coat sleeves, and then he entered my house and without warning he acted almost hamstrung, there was certainly suddenly something wrong with his knees, which buckling, brought him to sit down before I could invite him.

"Quintus Isham Pearch." Our visitor stretched out his

hands toward my applicant, and then gave a half-lunge up from the chair as Quintus cautiously drew near him.

"Dear son," the visitor continued, not quite risen up from the chair, "I am the Reverend Spinney from Three Oaks . . ."

As Quintus gazed fearful at the Reverend struggling to rise from his half-sitting position, my own sorrows all sort of vanished, for I could presage what was about to overtake him as one foresees the bad ocean storm that is to come from some tiny little warning, like the way a spider weaves its web.

"I have tried repeatedly to reach you for days . . . I had no idea indeed you had left home and mother . . ."

Reverend Spinney had now risen to his full height, and towered above Quintus in a wavering toppling manner. He folded his arms and his mouth set hideously.

In considerable confusion I sat down and motioned Quintus to do the same in the little chair beside me, which he gradually was able to do.

The Reverend from his finally achieved height gave me one sweep of a look as if to be sure he had seen me right the first time on the front porch, he stopped short again after this examination of my countenance, cleared his throat, and then leaning over Quintus and touching his forehead got out, "I am the bearer of the saddest news one man can impart to another. Your beloved mother is dead. We have translated her remains from the Heytesbury Funeral Parlor to her own domicile, where we have been so long awaiting you, her only son and heir. The services will begin, Quintus Isham," he disentangled his left hand from his right, drew out a timepiece which might almost have passed for an alarm clock for all the noise it made when out of his shiny purple-black vest pocket, "services due to start at twelve noon this day."

I remembered what Quintus had read to me then about the fact that at twelve noon we have no shadow and it is then that the Power of Evil has jurisdiction over us, and I looked over at him, but his face had a sort of grin on it which cut me, for I knew what a grin like that really means, and what he also was in store for.

Reverend Spinney looked away briefly from the bereaved son to half-look at me, almost as if he knew what I was thinking about.

"Shall we pray then, gent'men?" The preacher bowed his head, and waited, but only Quintus got up, and kneeled down, and the Reverend waited a bit more and then realizing, I guess, I wasn't going to follow suit spoke on the subject of how short a day we have, like the flowers, quick to bloom, quick to be cut down, and so on. I don't recollect what else he said because I was still too provoked by the way the Reverend had walked right in my house like he was accustomed to visiting, and his easy familiarity made me especially touchy because it looked like I was going to lose my property, and who knows, maybe this black Reverend was going to buy it out from my hands, but then my attention was brought back to Quintus. His whole body was shaking like he had malaria, and the Reverend irritated me still more then because he did not seem to notice the state Quintus was in, but then all of a sudden while my mind had been on something else Quintus was standing up and talking, saying, *"I don't know if I can attend the services at such short notice, Reverend. You see . . ."*

"Why, whatever do you mean by that, son?" the Reverend Spinney wondered, throwing his head way back and letting us see a set of teeth entirely gold through his open mouth.

"My friend Garnet here," Quintus turned to me and I only needed to give him one glance to know he was never going to be the same boy again, "my friend here is near . . . near . . . Garnet is a very sick man, Rev . . . He's a vet, you know, and has nobody to tend him . . ."

"I'll go with you to your mother's funeral, Quintus, so don't worry any . . ."

I went off then into the back part of my house, and let him take leave of the preacher. I fished out a bottle of bonded rye up from a cupboard nobody knew about and then I walked on out again past Quintus, acting as if I didn't notice how he was shaking even more now that the Rev had gone, and I got some ice, and brought him a big tumbler full of liquor, and handed it to him.

"You ought to let it all out, Quints," I said after he had swallowed a big mouthful. "Don't hold back your grief."

"You can't go to the funeral," Quintus said.

"Why can't I?" I turned on him scolding.

"Can you?" He sort of grinned with the new expression on his face. The whites of his eyes was red like someone had swatted him with a towel, but there was no water in them.

We took the bottle of rye along in case one of us (this was my idea) was taken bad, I wasn't sure which one would be first, and we got into my used cream-colored Oldsmobile, and we drove to Three Oaks, which though not too far is a place I had never been to. Actually, all it amounts to is a gasoline station, a church, four houses, a silo, a big field of something wavy and green growing, and this Civil War cemetery full of blacks they claim fought on the side of the Confederacy.

Quintus' mother's house was the best house of the four. They had black crêpe all over the pillars, there was gladiolus on the front porch in big silver vases, an American flag waving, and inside in the front sitting room was the orange casket, and lots of white-haired black ladies in big hats sitting on camp stools.

Quintus didn't greet anybody, and motioned me to follow him into one of the rooms off the hall. I could see by the way he didn't speak to anybody what I had feared from the first might happen, that is he would go all to pieces, and I hoped to God I would not have one of my spells and let both of us down. If only he would cry, he might get through the funeral, but no he wouldn't. So I made him drink some more of the rye right from the bottle, and then we went back to the mourning room and sat down on camp stools.

"Quintus," I said after having started to speak twenty times, "you have got to go up and look at your ma in the casket, you can't just sit here with me a stranger."

"By and by," he said.

My eye was running over the flowers, which I guess had been mostly sent by white folks his mother had worked for all her life, and all of a sudden I saw this big bouquet of roses and lilies with the card *Georgina Rance, with deepest sympathy*.

While the choir in the back of the house was singing one of the many hymns they comforted us with, without a word, I sort of lifted Quintus up by his arm pits, and then led him up to his mother's casket. Everybody else had their eyes closed in prayer, they didn't appear to notice. Quintus looked down on his mother's face, but he couldn't look more than once, and he took hold of my hand as if he was falling from a precipice, it was that kind of grip, and we went back to the camp stools.

I think we was in that room for four hours, only it seemed fifty, but gradually sort of, to my relief, though I knew this augured ill, Quints got just like a rag doll, I never saw anybody change so, and his forehead which had been as smooth as a sheet that morning suddenly was wrinkled and careworn like an old man of eighty. So gradually, but with all kinds of queer feelings, but not knowing what else to do, and afraid he would keel over without I did it, in front of everybody I took his right hand in my right hand

82

and held it tight as I could against my breast and I sensed he appreciated and wanted this, well, after all he had been rubbing my feet and waiting on me and reading to me all these past weeks, and he was the only one who had never cared that I looked like death itself.

But at the graveside, after the Reverend Spinney had read those most terrible words, words I never knew or had forgot that human beings would say to one another in public, such as we are short in time in this life and cut down like grass, are only after all a shadow and dust to dust and ashes to ashes, and then they threw clods of earth on the coffin, and afterwards, Quintus would not get into the car and be driven to my house or his, and I was thinking *lucky Quintus*, at least they are not going to foreclose on him, when all at once I realized what had happened, the day was coming to a close and the funeral party had finally give up and left us behind in the cemetery because he would not go with the funeral party, and then at last it happened, so I could relax a little myself, he was crying and hollering like a wild man, his spit flying out from his wide-open mouth, kneeling on his mother's fresh-dug grave, for he could be himself alone with me, he didn't mind saying or doing anything around me. I let him scream and holler for a long time, and when his tears came, I let them gush and rush and flow for as long as I thought it did him any good. Then I went up to him and kneeled also on the grave, and he tried to turn his face away from me, as if it still had any secret from me, and I slapped him a little, and then harder, I brought his shoulders up square and looked at his closed eyes with the eyelashes as wet as a drowned animal's fur, and I brought out the bottle of rye which was getting ever so little low, and said, *"Come on now, Quints, put this between your teeth now."*

"Oh, Daventry, a heavy blow has fallen upon our house, which nobody could have foresaw!"

I said this upon reading the eviction notice again from the sheriff after we was home from Quint's ma's funeral.

"What do you want to call on him for," Quintus wondered, "when here he stole your girl from you . . . ?"

"Well, let me see . . . Why do I call on him . . . ? You think he's a pretty bad character, do you . . . ?"

"Oh, I don't know. Anyhow he took your girl from you."

"Well, I pushed him over the precipice though . . . He didn't want to go to her . . . But the thing I hold against him most is he discovered my secret."

Quintus watched me from the kitchen where he had sat down by the calendar, one of those big shiny things with pictures of Bible characters in robes which was put out by a company that sells chicken feed.

"We have to have all the furniture out of this house by next Tuesday so that the dispossession can take place," I reminded him, walking out into the kitchen to say this, and then walking back into the sitting room.

"What secret are you talking about?" Quintus' voice sounded sort of sly, and I was glad to note he didn't speak so sobby and bawling anymore. I believe, as a matter of fact, I was feeling worse by now than he, but I always feel worse than anybody else on account of I'm not supposed to be among the living at all, or as the doc always kept harping, *"Consider it like this, you were spared by some unexplained breaking of natural laws."*

I could have bitten my tongue off now for ever mentioning it in the first place. The secret, I mean.

"Oh, forget it, Quints," I flared up as he asked again what it was. "Let's think about dispossession . . ."

Quintus had changed all right since the funeral. I knew he would never be the same as before with me because something had happened between us from the moment old Reverend Spinney materialized to give us the bad news, and then something had happened as we sat in the little room next to his mother's coffin. Put it like this, we had a claim on one another from that time on.

"I thought you would want to share everything that bothered you with me," Quintus said. "That's what you said when you was so sick one night . . ."

"That so?" I mumbled. Had I been able to blush I would have then.

"O.K. That was in delirium though, I reckon, Quints," I said after a few moments' thought.

"What's the difference, Garnet?" That was the first time he ever called me by my Christian name.

"Well, see here, Quints. If you don't know the difference between delirium . . . and . . ." But I stopped because I felt he was right, at least in my case there is no difference. I have gone through so many dark valleys there just is no difference . . .

"All right, Quints, now you spill it . . ."

"Just know that I know, Garnet . . ."

"All right, what do you know? . . . That I killed a hundred men . . . That I harbor a desperado here under my dispossessed roof, who took my girl . . . That I am a dead man who goes on living . . . Come on, spill my secret . . ."

"Don't you bait me, Garnet, or I'll go home for good now . . ."

Of course he was not serious, but what he had said struck me. This Quintus had a roof and a home he could go to, and I would soon be lower than white trash, certainly lower than any black man around here, because my land would be gone . . .

He came over to the chair I was sitting in now and watched me.

"You all right, Garnet?"

"Yeah, Garnet is all right. After all, I can't die, can I, so how can I be but all right . . . ? If you don't tell me my secret, though, pretty damn quick you may be my hundred-and-first victim . . ."

He sat down in his old lazy-bones loose-jointed way and began unlacing my shoes.

"Will you let me rub your feet, Quintus, after I am dispossessed?" I inquired.

"Oh, I might oblige you on that score, Garnet."

Quintus was already rubbing my feet but with an absentminded sober look on his face that was new to him.

I touched the hair of his head for the first time, and he jumped.

"Tell me what you know, Quints."

"Daventry don't love the Widow . . ."

"Oh no? But he lays her just the same according to you . . ."

"It ain't love."

"All right, what's my secret if you know so damn much?"

"I ain't the only one who knows now, mind you," Quintus began. "Say, your feet ain't so cold today, you must be improving your circulation."

"I never knew you to tease before, Quints." I was touching his hair still more partly through astonishment at how much bear grease he must have put on it that day, but he jerked away from me as though my hands disgusted him.

"Do you want me to read to you now?" He had put back on my shoes and socks.

"I want to hear you tell me you know what I keep secret, you know that."

"All right! All right for you! Daventry and me followed you one night."

I closed my eyes and pushed myself away from him. Then I buckled up like I had appendicitis, only I believe it hurt me more.

"We followed you," he went on, "slow oh so slow up the cliffs and down past little creeks and junglelike places and unused cowpaths and all, well you know the way after all, and then we seen you go into . . ."

". . . The dance hall . . ."

". . . Which I never knowed existed anymore and I born and bred here . . . Yeah . . ." Quintus grabbed my left foot and pulled it over to him and began rubbing the calf, and held it even though I tried to get out of his grasp . . .

"We watched you through the windows . . ."

I groaned and cursed like he was tearing out my guts.

"We seen you dance with yourself under that revolving . . .

". . . Moon."

"Well, that ain't what it's called, but if you say so, all right, *moon.* You looked good though under those little polka-dot lights revolving all over you . . . You looked like a fine young white man."

"Sure, shit."

"We was both impressed, Daventry and me. Only Daventry began to bawl. That was when I found out about him."

"That he was wanted . . ."

"Cripes no, Garnet, desperado, wanted, nothing . . . Daventry turned to me and said, '*I love Garnet. I've loved him from the minute I seen him. I never want to leave him.*'"

"Quintus," I started, and I grabbed him by both his ears and held his eyes right up almost to mine, don't you bullshit me now, after all I've gone through . . ."

Quintus breaknecked away from me, and standing up said, "Why don't you listen to anything I ever say to you . . . ? That's why I have to read to you because you won't never listen . . ."

"All right." I began trying to think it over. "He seen me dancing under that moon that gives off polka-dot lights, all right . . ."

"Well, I've told you everything then . . . We know your secret . . ."

"And you still want to be friends with me, is that it?"

Quintus stared at me, if not dumbfounded, considerably nonplussed.

"But your other . . . statement, Quints, must be some barefaced lie to make me feel bad down deep . . ."

"What statement you mean?" He would not help me.

"You said Daventry loved me." It took everything out of me to say this.

"That's what he said, yes. He said you was his other self, and he would never part with you."

And speaking of the devil, there he come in the front door, Daventry. He looked a lot younger. Well, he had a new suit of clothes on, and this new pink shirt.

"What's this I hear about you bein' dispossessed and evicted by the sheriff?" He went straight to the point and came over to where I was half-falling out of my chair.

"Why, they can't do that to you, Garnet . . . I won't allow them . . ."

"Yeah," I said, but avoiding his face as much as I used to think he had avoided mine.

"No, siree," Daventry said. "I won't allow them to throw you out. And you a war hero and all, just let them try . . ."

"Where are those dispossess papers, by the way?"

Daventry wondered, and seeing them on my little spinet desk he gathered them up, and also seeing Quintus' dime-store reading specs he took them up also and put them on his nose but didn't like them and laid them down.

He studied the papers a long long time, while I studied him.

"Were you a sheep-farmer yourself?" I said out of the blue.

He looked up quick from the papers. "My dad was," he replied.

"Well, then you must have been too, wasn't you? I mean you must know all about sheep, even if you ain't what would be called today a shepherd."

I was smoking some of his grass now, and he noticed this.

"Well, nobody called my dad a shepherd," he spoke emphatically, and he began marking little sections of the dispossess papers with a stub of a Mohawk pencil.

"But you lived around sheep," I had to go on. "Did you have sheep dogs?"

Both Quintus and Daventry looked at me somewhat cautious, puzzled, and a little concerned.

"Why all at once do you want me to tell you about my life in Utah, Garnet?"

"I hear you been spying on me in your spare time." I brought this up now, for my secret having been discovered upset me almost more than anything since the day I found out I would never look like I belonged among the living again, that my inside was my outside, etc.

Daventry looked at Quintus as if he could have killed him, so I said quickly, "Quintus' mother has passed away, and we have been to the funeral."

"Oh, Quints." Daventry got up right away and went over to him. "I'm grieved to hear that." He tried to take Quintus' hand, but I guess I am the only white man Quintus ever let touch him, come to think of it, so Daventry had to just pat his shoulder four or five times.

"So I hope you're satisfied, Daventry." I went back to my secret, and I believe the grass was doing something to me now.

"Satisfied as to what?" His voice sounded like a big orchestra of trumpets so that I thought I was going deaf. He stood of course right by me.

"What are you so interested all of a sudden in me being a shepherd for?" he thundered. "Hey?"

"Your dad is the shepherd, ain't it?" I got out. I felt I was going to bawl, so I handed him the joint.

"There ain't no shepherds, only ranchers," Daventry appealed to Quintus in his growing dismay.

"Well, you slept with my girl and you found out I have this secret place I go to. The ruined dance hall of course is what I mean, with the polka-dot lights. You've got everything I have. I also understand you are in love with me, though I don't quite know what you mean by that."

Daventry looked so confounded, I've never seen a white man look so at sea before, he looked as if he was going to shake his arms and legs off of him the way he flailed around. He would look at Quintus and then at me, and then he would look down at the dispossession papers which he held still in his right hand.

Finally he sat very deliberately down on the floor, and put his head between his knees.

"Is there anything more I have or maybe don't have that you want, Daventry?" I inquired. I don't know why I was being so mean to him.

"I don't really love the Widow Rance, as you call the bitch," he said.

"But you went to bed with her, didn't you?" I said, and the thought of it made me so dizzy I had to hold my own head between my knees at once to keep from keeling over (one of my doc's many remedies to keep me among the living or at least the conscious, and as a matter of fact I spent most of my time in the hospital with my head between my legs, it did seem).

"Now you see here, God damn it," Daventry began, looking up, and *had his face changed*. Both Quintus and me was hushed to see it. "You look here, will you," he began, and the spit began to form on his lips like foam. "You set me up with her! You wanted this to happen, and you know it. You made me the bearer of those messages. I never wanted to go near her. Never even heard tell of her. You set me up."

He looked so wild then and I remembered he was after all maybe a murderer. But I didn't care, and had he meant to kill me I wouldn't have put up a fight to save myself.

"Sure she's beautiful, sure she's luscious, sure she's like a ripe cherry and all those things Quintus reads to you out of books . . . But I don't want her, but I had to do it with her because I thought it was your command. Do you hear that? So I did it with her. Again and again, and then some. I am wore out from it, I can tell you. She hasn't had any loving for so long she can't remember when, and it all had to come from out of me . . ."

His countenance had changed so much that neither Quintus nor me would have recognized him by his face alone, but we might have by his long yellow hair and the way he talked.

"She thinks you don't like her," he said after a while, which was the most astonishing thing I had heard yet. I laughed a little when he said it.

"Then," he went on, but looking down at the dispossession papers, "as to spying on you, that's a damned dirty fucking lie and you know it. We followed you because we was worried about you. Not to get anything on you. After all, Garnet, I have leveled with you, told you I am a wanted man and all, but I killed in self-defense, and on my dad's land. And finally," he said, and he was beginning to bawl now, and the spit from his lips flying in every which way, "this little traitor of a Quintus telling tales out of school. Well maybe I said I did love you, so what? Is that any crime . . . ?"

"But what do you mean by it, Daventry?" I said in a soft voice, but any voice the sound only of a tiny locust leaf blowing through the soft summer air would have been too loud at that moment, for the next second he was at my throat, strangling me, and shouting, "What do you think I meant by it, damn you, can't I love somebody without me being put on trial for murder?"

He let loose of me almost immediately then, as I guess he more than realized I had such a thin tie holding me to this world anyhow.

"I'll pack and leave now," he said quietly and went off into his part of the house to get ready.

I knew then that if I didn't get up I would never get up again, I knew then though my pride had never been so high, and my spirit so ignoble, I knew if he went I would, yes, I would die at last, and though I wanted to die I didn't want to die without him, all because mostly of that speech he had just made, no, it was all of him, from the moment I seen him with his yellow hair and no front teeth and his sweet smile looking at me from the jungle of trees, I even liked, to tell the truth, the way he had vomited when he took me in the first time.

He was tying a bandana around his neck when I got into the room, but he never once looked at me. I went up to him several times, but he paid no more attention to me than if I was his shadow or the hollyhock bush that was looking through the window at him. I fell at his knees not because I had planned to go down on my knees before him, I was as a matter of fact passing out, and knelt to break my fall, but I knew I had to say what I had to say, for if I didn't I would be done for, so I said, *"Don't you ever leave me, Daventry."*

"How's this?" he said, his savage face bearing down on me, and I knew then he had killed.

"You forgive me before you go, but if you go, Daventry,

94

I think my heart will break. Don't forgive me if you don't want to. All I said to you was a lie."

"A lie, huh, yeah for once you said it. Worst lie I ever heard."

He was looking though at Quintus, who had followed us on back and who I could kind of feel was even more troubled now than when he had been at his own ma's funeral.

"Don't go and leave him, Daventry," Quintus spoke up. "You can't desert him now," he pleaded.

"You know my secret," I spoke up, "you know you do."

He had just turned to look at me when this new hemorrhage came out of both my ears at the same time, and he and Quintus started toward me, but I didn't want them to do anything because the pressure that had been building up in my head was leaving me, and all the blood pouring out gave me such a good free feeling just then.

"It's all right, I can tell I'm all right," I told them, "Don't do nothing just yet. Just get cloths and clean up the mess." I leaned against the bed and watched them. "But don't let Daventry out of the house, you hear," I addressed Quintus, "don't let him . . ."

Shortly afterwards when everything quieted down I heard Daventry playing the mouth-organ. Quintus was sitting by me looking through a set of old seed catalogues he had found in the attic, trying to decide, I guess, if he could find anything particular to read to me after what had occurred, and he had begun a few times to read little bits and pieces of paragraphs, like one I remember even now:

"Varieties of wheat are not the same everywhere, and where they are the same they do not always bear the same names. The most widely known are common wheat and hard wheat . . ."

I motioned for Quintus to be silent, for what I was hearing was too beautiful. I knowed what it was and I didn't. It was my mouth-organ of course which Daventry had found and which I hadn't played for so long, long before I went into the army, but hear how he played it! He made it sound almost like a flute. I remember too he was playing "On the Alamo."

Quintus went on pretending he was reading now to himself, but his eyes didn't really move from one side of the page to the other, and I knew he was listening.

When Daventry stopped playing we clapped. He came out of the bedroom grinning to beat the band.

But as I turned away from him owing to being so moved, my face all wreathed in smiles at the hearing of how he could turn an old harmonica into a beautiful solo instrument and about to congratulate him through my embarrassment and happiness, who do I see but a man at the side door who I recognize as the sheriff.

I got up and went out to speak to him.

The sheriff had some more of these legal papers, and I was about to take them from his hand when another hand snatched them from out my grasp. It was Daventry of course.

"Now you look here, officer . . ."

I marveled so at him talking up to the law like that when here he must be wanted in I don't know how many states, or on the other hand, I thought, still marveling at him, maybe he ain't wanted nowhere, and this talk of him being a murderer is one of his tales, for I was pretty sure by then Daventry was crazy.

When I left for the Army I did not know one crazy person, but while I was in service I got to know enough for several lifetimes, I got to know more than most doctors ever know in their lives unless they are crazy-specialists. But Daventry was crazy in a way you will never find in any other man. He was divine-crazy or heaven-crazy, I mean God had touched him, for instance when he said he loved me I knew what he meant, but I wanted to play the part of an ordinary soldier from Virginia and spurn him, when the truth of it was I loved him from the beginning but my deformity, my being turned inside out would not allow me at first to see he loved me for what I am. I knew then there was God, and that Daventry had been sent for me, and I knew also he would leave me. That is why I didn't care anything about what the sheriff said, and this puzzled Daventry, for he knew he was going to leave me, but he wanted me to be left in a safe quiet place, but I didn't care any more. Of course I still loved the Widow Rance, Georgina, would always love her, but Daventry was more. When he played the harmonica I knew he was not human.

"You've got to fight for your house and land," Daventry was haranguing me. Our quarrel had long blown over of course. "You can't let them put you out on the big road with your furniture, Garnet. You served your country. They can't do this to you. Now you listen to me . . ."

He told me the strategy we were to take, he mentioned the names of Mrs. Gondess and I heard the sheriff's surname several times (Mr. Hespe), but I had taken to smoking his grass more than I should have at this time and didn't pay close attention, which annoyed him.

"Can't you do anything with this son of a bitch?" Daventry finally appealed to Quintus.

"I can't and I won't," Quintus replied, still poring over another catalogue he was stuck on at the moment concerning crops and animal husbandry.

"Then there's nothing to do but put all his furniture out by the side of the road, for tomorrow they're coming in . . . Unless I can think up something, that is . . ."

Daventry's attention was very gradually and slowly diverted to a recent local newspaper that had been allowed to lie undisturbed and unread on the carpet. His gaze gradually became riveted to something in it, maybe a headline. He stooped down to pick it up oh so slow, like he had found a telegram there from his sheriff. I can still see the expression on his face as he looked at something that was printed there and which he roved his eye over in astonished disbelief. I could see his lips move as he took in the print, and then he looked up at me, dropping the paper, as if he had found something published there that I had said against him.

"Now look here, Garnet, why didn't you tell me?" he spoke, and I felt indeed as if they had put something in the newsprint I had said in his disfavor, that maybe it was claimed I had reported he was a desperado.

Going back to the paper and reading more, he then looked up again and exclaimed, "Well, I'll be damned . . . Is this true?"

Even Quintus looked up and gave his undivided attention.

"You mean to tell me you have hurricanes here?" Daventry accused us.

He acted as affronted as if I had invited him down here to Virginia, had given him his job, and then had withheld this sensitive information.

"Don't they have hurricanes just about everywhere, Daventry," I replied, for I was more than dumbfounded by the way in which he was plainly holding me accountable for this.

"And it's expected in a few days, they claim!" He threw the paper in my direction.

"Oh, those weather forecasts," I scoffed. "Why, you can't go by them. They have them *around* here, bad storms of course, sure, but we never get hurricanes Daventry . . ."

"You don't care about anything!" he vociferated. "Your girl Georgina, your hemorrhaging (here I gave him a rather nasty look), the sheriff, losing your land and home when as that old rip from the Real Estate Office said your family goes way back to the beginnings of this country. You just don't care, Garnet . . ."

"I care about your harmonica playing, Daventry."

"Oh well, yes I suppose you do . . . But why oh why,

Garnet, didn't you tell me about the hurricanes . . . ?"

Both Quintus and I just stared at him point-blank.

"Just the name *hurricane* scares me to death. I can't bear it!"

He got up and went over to the big window that looks out on the ocean side. I guess he was looking at the ocean (which he had never seen before till he visited us) for it to give him maybe a weather forecast.

I went over to him then and looked at the expanse of blue-green sea also. It was still and smooth and to tell the truth didn't look like itself. It looked like a field.

"Why, Daventry," I tried to comfort him, "we folks here don't think about the hurricanes. If one does come, which ain't probable, you can't do anything about it anyhow, can you? It's no worse than floods. Don't you have floods in Utah?"

He shook his head and moved away from me.

"Or cyclones or tornadoes?"

He went on gazing out the window in the direction of the quiet sea.

The day we were to be evicted had come at last. We had put some more of my grandfather's furniture out by the side of the road, more commodes, china closets, Circassian walnut beds nobody had slept in since before I was born, and a long maple dining table that must have seated twenty-five people. We didn't move yet our beds or the hundreds and hundreds of books. We were planning to move some of my things to Quintus' ma's house if the worst came to the worst, but he wasn't too sure if he was going to be allowed to live there on account of the will had not been opened yet and studied because the lawyer lived in Richmond. Some people said his ma was well off on account of she had worked for rich white people for thirty years.

"I am going to save you," Daventry said, coming up to me where I was seated near the gas range in the kitchen. He looked mad as a farm of hornets. His eyes barely focused and I think if I had been really afraid of anybody anymore I would have been afraid of him at that moment. There were little thick pearls of sweat on his upper lip.

"If you will let me," he went on, "I will save you. I will do it, but I may never be the same again. Is that understood?"

He walked about the room like a man standing on red-hot coals.

"There is no other way but to do what I am going to do," he spoke, really I suppose to himself. "I prayed all night," he now came up to me, "but it didn't work."

I remembered then how he had tossed and turned all night in the bed next to me. Actually I don't think I ever sleep. I get a little quiet sometimes and my eyes are closed most of the time anyhow, or off and on closed at any rate. At the same time ever since I was blown up with my buddies I have never felt really wide awake either. I bet that they lying in in those far-off untended graves by the

South China seas are about as wide awake as me most of the time.

"Do you have any wine, Quintus?" Daventry turned to him now rather than me. Quintus begrudged giving up reading even for a minute, but he let him know there was a bottle of Virginia Dare in the cupboard, and so Daventry brought this out. It was a good thing I didn't know what was coming, or I think I would have run as far away as Utah myself at that moment. I am trying to recollect it, for I think it was in a way the most horrible thing that ever happened to me.

"Do you have big tin cups like they use on farms?" he then wondered.

Quintus finally rose then for he felt something serious was in the offing, as I gradually did, and he got him a cup.

"I need three," Daventry said sharply.

He meanwhile uncorked the wine.

Looking at his eyes I felt he must have taken some pill or drug, for his eyes didn't look anymore like his than a tiger's, the pupils were coming out of him like big black beads from a busted necklace. Both Quintus and me were getting terribly uneasy and was looking toward the doors like for escape.

"*I will save your land and property, if you will commune with me.*" Daventry spoke these words solemnly and in a voice that sounded like he was talking behind a blanket. It suddenly got more churchlike too in the kitchen than even the funeral of Quintus' mother.

Very gradually we all sat down at the table with our

tin cups in front of us and wonder of wonders Daventry
closed his eyes and began intoning. My lower lip shook so
bad I had to hold it still with my fingers.

I was about to say it's all right for them to foreclose on
us, but it was too late.

I saw the knife, and I saw his chest bare without his shirt
anywhere in evidence. He had the most beautiful chest of
any man I have ever seen, and no wonder Georgina had to
have him—if he was that beautiful all over, she was right.

I didn't exactly see him slash himself, but saw the blood
first spurt and spray all over the table, but he had self-
command enough to fill each tin cup with the jetting stream
of his blood. Quintus sort of lay back in his chair and his
arms got loose like they was made of straw.

But each of the tin cups had been filled with blood and
wine, and the look on Daventry's face was so fearful, and
the knife resting in his left hand so fierce, there was nothing to do when he said *"Drink"* but swallow it, and I decided of course he was going to kill us then too and though
I was trembling like a young quail when it's picked up
from its covey, I was ready for whatever he had to pro-
pound for us, and Daventry was, I guess, the person I had
always been seeking, he could make me obey, he had come
too late of course, but if he was to lead me out of my
perplexities and sorrows into the next kingdom, well and
good.

That was when time stopped.

I don't think it was the grass. Was it the blood? It
couldn't have been that old wine.

No, I seemed to have been sitting with Daventry and Quintus four thousand years around that table with the tin cups and the boy with all that blood on his chest and side.

Finally I could see it was dark outside, and raining.

We were to have been evicted at ten o'clock that morning and it was now God knows what time. The clock in the front sitting room registered twelve, and so that must mean midnight judging by the darkness outside. There that good furniture stood too out there all by itself on the side of the road, getting all wet and damaged. I went out and started to fetch some of it in.

"He's delirious," Quintus told me as I was dragging in a big chest of drawers.

I went into the room and looked at him. We had bandaged his chest and side where he had slashed himself. I caught a sudden glimpse of myself in the mirrror. I have never seen such a face. There was blood on my mouth and chin, but looking a bit closer I did not think I looked so horrible as usual, I mean I looked sort of almost human. I studied myself though only a split second for I had to tend to Daventry now.

"*We wasn't evicted.*" I spoke this to Quintus after another long spell of time had passed. He was reading as usual, but he read silently now, hardly ever giving me any of his information.

He took off his glasses and stared at me.

"Maybe the sheriff will come tomorrow," he suggested.

"Did you ever hear of an eviction that didn't take place?

Huh-huh," I answered my own question. "There won't be any eviction. Something's changed . . ."

As I sat by his bed, he sort of come to gradually and said in a hoarse changed voice . . . *"Garnet?"*

"I'm right beside you, Daventry."

"You didn't vomit up any of my blood, did you?" he questioned.

As he said this I did turn quite nauseous and began to retch, and he sprung up out of bed like a wildcat and pressed his hand against my lips, so that whatever the liquid was that was spoiling to come out would go back into me.

"You mustn't lose a drop, Garnet . . . I have saved you, I believe. Wish I could save myself . . ."

"Can't I save you?"

"No, you can't, Garnet."

The wind had come up and he listened to it so carefully. He listened to the wind in a way like Quintus read books, like he had already understood what the wind was saying before he began to listen.

"Daventry, you are a messenger, aren't you?" I don't know why I said this, and I don't know what I meant when I said it. Often though I do say things, they come out of me, like Daventry's blood tried to come out from my mouth, and the words have a meaning, but I don't know what they signify. As Daventry said once later on before

he left us for good, *"Garnet, you are a vessel in which is flowing the underground river of life."*

"Oh, that wind, that wind!" he cried.

"It's not a hurricane," I comforted him.

"But it's wind." He shook his head mournfully. I never heard such a terrible wind.

"It'll stop in a little while," I tried to comfort him. "Don't listen to it meanwhile . . ."

"Why, what was that?" He suddenly let out a cry and took hold of my shoulder blade with a grip of iron. "What is it?"

I had to listen myself very carefully for you see I am so used to all the sounds around here and pay no special mind to them, whilst Daventry coming from so far off, practically the South China seas, is aware of and studies every little whichever noise.

"That awful sound like a lion or an elephant!" And he raised his right hand upwards.

"Daventry, you do surprise me. That's the ocean you hear, that's the ocean's own voice."

His face relaxed in a grin. "Oh go on with you," he quipped. "I guess I walked into that one."

"Well, he is trumpeting and hollering a lot . . ."

Everything indeed shook, everything trembled, and then everything got deathly quiet, except for the ocean, which still moaned and hammered on the sand, and splashed and howled and then sort of whined even, and kept beating.

He was looking at my mouth and I got un uneasy feeling again. He picked up a box of kleenex, wetted a sheet of it with his own mouth, and wiped my mouth off, I don't know what it had on it he felt it should be cleaned, I dared not ask.

"Will you remember me as much as you do your buddies who was with you in the war?" he inquired.

I was so terribly moved my tongue clove to the roof of my mouth.

He didn't ask the question again. I wanted to tell him I would remember him forever, nobody had ever impressed me like Daventry, but I could not say a thing, for if I had spoken I would have vomited, and he had forbid that.

Then the first thing I knew I was looking out the window, and the sun was coming up like a gold watch over the stilled ocean.

I always got up earlier than either Quintus or Daventry because I am the light sleeper.

I was drinking this cup of strong coffee, with a little fresh honey in it, when I saw the mailman get out of his delivery truck, and take out a big letter which he peered down at and which I later discovered had a special delivery stamp on it.

I watched the mailman walk up the front path, from the road, and then I jumped up and walked out to meet him halfway for I didn't want him to wake my applicants.

"Couldn't get here yesterday night on account of the

storm," the mailman began. Actually all he was doing was staring at all my furniture by the roadside, its heirloom wood ruined by wet.

The special delivery was from Mrs. Gondess, and I opened it in front of the mailman because to tell the truth I thought this was what you were supposed to do.

It was a cold, disappointed letter, informing me that all my back taxes had been paid by a Veterans Organization in Richmond, who had heard of my hard-pressed situation. Mrs. Gondess said she hoped I would have learned from this harrowing experience in which I had put everybody including myself to such hardship and worry.

"You would judge," I began, looking from the mailman to the ruined wood of my grandfather's furniture, "that we was about to have an auction. Fact is though we ain't, not now anyhow . . ."

He began to move off in the direction of his truck, but I detained him with, "Do you think," I put to him, as his eye roved over the wet commodes and bedsteads and chiffoniers, "that anybody ever learns from experience?" . . . a question that was prompted by Mrs. Gondess' letter of course.

The mailman grinned. "By the time," he said, "you've learned from one experience you're up against some new one with no experience to help you with it, and so you make all the same mistakes again only in a new setting . . ."

I went on studying my special-delivery letter.

"His shed blood turned the trick," I said. I got cold all over and I realized I was going to have an attack.

The next thing I knew I was lying under two hand-sewn quilts from Quintus' ma's house. They were so silk-smooth and quite beautiful but covered with the sweat that poured down from me. I forget whether I have mentioned that I have contracted at least two strains of malaria that don't have no cure in this country, and I have another strain that sort of responds to quinine.

It was night again by now, so that day beginning when I had read the letter had just vanished away like the dew, and Quintus was poking me in the ribs, and he had to repeat the thing he was saying several times: "*She is outside a-asking to talk with you.*"

I knew who he meant so I didn't bother to reply. At first I thought I would act cute and say "*Mrs. Gondess?*" but I knew that old harridan-hellion would never darken my door again unless she could dispossess me for sure of course. No, I knew who *she* was. There was only one *she* in my life anyhow, and she is everywhere. But it did fell me more or less that she had come to see me in her own person.

The Widow Rance stood before me then in a big shimmering cloak people wear around here in hurricane season. She removed it, and was in her creamy summer dress.

I had just enough strength to motion her to sit down beside me.

I don't know if she looked at my face or not. There was

nothing else of me to look at for my hands and body were wrapped in Quintus' ma's quilts.

I guess she looked more beautiful than ever, but I got to thinking that if you could forget his vacant teeth, Daventry was possessed of a better complexion and his hair would have graced Absalom of old. But of course she was the beautiful woman of this vicinity, only she was after all, I realized now, just human.

"Well, Georgina," I said, "so you have humbled yourself this much . . ."

"I would apologize, Garnet, if I could. I know I have not been good to you. And I thank you, if I haven't said so before, for all you did for this country."

"Hollow," I said. I had just about enough strength to say it.

"I have also kept your letters," she proceeded, "because they are from a hero."

"That ain't any reason for even readin' them. I didn't write them to you as a hero."

"However that may be, Garnet," she continued, lowering those long gorgeous eyelashes and folding her shell-pink hands that had never done any more work than rinse out her breakfast dishes or maybe shake out a tiny rug . . . "I have come here to ask you a favor," she finished.

"And that is?"

"I know, Garnet, I deserve your contempt and coldness, but pray, for what you felt for me before you went so far away and fought for us all . . ."

Here of course she began to bawl, but I was a stone wall to tears by now.

"You know I think, Garnet, what has happened . . ."

"Speak your piece, Georgina, speak it out . . ." I was able to say that much by rising up to a sitting position, after which exertion I plumped back onto the pillow cases.

"Daventry told me that I would require . . . your permission if not your blessing . . ."

"Aha," I grinned.

"So I have come for that permission, for oh, Garnet, I do love him so very much . . . But he will not leave you without your blessing."

"Daventry is welcome to you," I said. "And it."

"You won't turn against him when he is mine?"

I couldn't speak now. I think I may have wanted to, but you see my strength had completely gone. I could not even call for Quintus.

"You might say," she reflected, her attention straying for a moment to take in a little path of day lilies outside that had run wild, "that I have come to ask his hand in marriage of you."

"Then take it, and take him," I told her.

"But you don't say it with your blessing."

"I bless him and all he does because he's blessed me . . . But beware," I warned her then.

"Don't say it," she begged me. "Just give me the right to marry him."

"I have been reading or had read to me," I began after I had calmed down a bit, "strange old books from my grand-father's library, Georgina . . . And we, that is Quints and me, has read there all sorts of prophecies, prognostications, forecasts and so on, and have consulted flowers and herbs, at least Quintus swears he has. Daventry too has looked into the eye of the future more than most . . ."

She was weeping hard now, a true picture of a woman in love. I wanted to hate her but I was too sick through and through. His blood maybe had curdled in me—anyhow I had not eat or drunk a thing since that terrible drink he give me.

"What I mean is," I consoled her, "enjoy him all you can, for the future is dark, do you mind me? . . . There ain't no future . . ."

"Oh, Garnet, bless you, bless you . . ."

"That's not needful, Widow Rance. I've been blessed already . . ."

She looked me full in the face, and then she got up and left.

She had only been gone the space of a few moments when I raised up with some difficulty, for I had not felt up to even my own morbid self after that ceremony with the tin cups and Daventry, and I run after her calling in a voice that made echoes all through the cliffs and little woodlands nearby *"Georgina! Wait up!"*

I had to hold on to one of the white cedar trees that grew along the shortcut to her house in order to get back my breath, and this time she waited as composed and tolerant as if I was the bridegroom or at least the desirable best man.

"I wanted you to know," I gasped out to her, "that it was Daventry who saved my house and land from being dispossessed . . . Don't ask me how he did it," I vetoed the questions that I saw beginning to form themselves on her mouth. "All I can say at this juncture is he did the trick that saved me . . . My house and land, you understand," I repeated . . .

Yes, she was sweet, yes she has luscious, yes she was so adorable, and then she was gone. I held on to the white cedar until I had a queer feeling I was part of its limbs and resin. It was more alive though than me, more knowing I do believe, and it had all its branches and sap.

Daventry spent more time with Georgina then, which was only to be expected since they were to be married, but come to think of it he didn't spend hardly any more time with her now than he had when he was a bearer of my messages. That is, he had always spent more time with her than maybe I was aware of . . . His betrothal brought about a change of course in our household, for the main task of it had been centered around my writing the letters to the Widow and having them sent by hand. The reading to me from old tomes by Quintus and sometimes by Daventry was actually only to get me warmed up to write the love letters. Now all this had changed. I wrote no more letters to anybody, and Quintus was more and more apt to read only to himself than read to me, and what he read was deeper and deeper as time went on, and he finally read from books that don't make any sense at all. Gradually I came to the realization that Quintus was either a whole sight smarter than me or else he was the damnedest play-actor that ever drew breath and understood even less of what he read than I did hearing, but the fact is I believe he understood more of it than I did, which is not to say he got much out of it but the labor.

The real billowing tossing part of Quintus' grief over his ma had subsided a little, but a kind of weighty eager restless something had settled over him now, his hands was too nervous to be satisfied anymore turning pages of books, his eyes didn't look the same, and there were little wrinkles around the corner of his mouth that wasn't there before, and his nose, which is a handsome nose stole from some English slave driver I reckon, looked thin and peaked. But I could tell even though I tried not even to say it to myself that he was going to run off and leave me too.

"Do you think, Quintus," I said to him one day cautious-cautious even to broach such a subject, "do you think now that what he done for us stopped the sheriff?"

"Daventry?" he replied knowing damn well who else did I mean by *he*.

He put his book down, and I picked it up and snorted. It was a history of weather.

"He is afraid of the wind, that's for sure." Quintus watched me leaf through his book.

"Quintus, why do you stay with me?" I said going back to something I felt in the air too, my fear now that he would leave me likewise.

He stirred and his nose moved down toward my hands clasped over the book which I had closed.

"Don't have nobody else to choose to stay with, guess," he mumbled.

"You don't feel looked down to and abused by me, like those newspapers you used to read against white people."

"Oh, I suppose I do. I suppose you're an enemy deep down and under, but I believe I told you the truth, there ain't nobody else to choose . . ."

"You stay with me then because I don't mean nothing to you one way or another."

"You mean a thing to me or so . . ." It took him a long time to get this said.

"Well, Daventry said he loved me." I picked my way through all this snaky labyrinth.

"I heard him."

"Couldn't you sort of care for me just a little?"

"I feel we are connected, Daventry. I feel we have been chose to be together for a while."

"Do you think Daventry was chose to come here . . . ?"

"I believe everything is chosen and destiny," he replied. He took the book out from my hands then and started off to the kitchen, his favorite site for reading.

"I'll be awful beside myself and lonesome when he is a married man." I raised my voice so it would reach the reader.

"You'll get over it," Quintus spoke through yawns. "I ain't going to leave you anyhow. Not just yet," he said and that *not just yet* went through me like a knife, it confirmed my fears, you see.

"I don't confess my love to folks, though," Quintus began like he was going to give a short speech, but then he stopped and said no more right then.

"Well, I care about you anyhow, Quintus . . . That's something Daventry taught me, I guess. I don't know what love means, but I think I am getting to have an inkling about it sometimes . . ."

Rocked in the boughs of slumber.

That is of course from one of those books Quintus, in his day, was constantly reading to me. So many phrases, parts of sentences, even paragraphs have stuck in my mind from those last days, Daventry's last days.

I remember those final few days mostly by sounds. Everything was sound. Daventry had taught me to listen to the winds and the ocean again. I had paid them no more attention than my own beating heart and pulsing arteries. But now I listened to the ocean. I knew he was angry. I knew the winds were not ordinary winds either. They ran like spirits in search of something. And the sky looked like lemon mixed with ashes. The moon was not right either. It looked like gray foam. And the birds, Daventry had wondered at their constant comment on everything from before dawn to our swift twilight. They were mostly silent, and they had lost a lot of their nests in the gales. A sandpiper was blown all the way from the ocean to our front porch, and had hurt its wing and breast, and I nursed it a while until one day it disappeared. One morning too I saw an eagle pursuing a waterbird, and both, I swear, dipped into the ocean and did not appear again.

But Daventry said nothing about the rising winds and the tides which he had worried so much about. He studied me a lot though.

Georgina was home getting ready her wedding dress. They had invited me to the ceremony, and its not being her first marriage by any means, not much was being done to inviting other people in, considering too the bridegroom was unknown in this community.

Then Quintus came in one day and said the kids and goats had disappeared. But Daventry made no comment on that or on most other things said, and was in a brown study, and his absentmindedness left me a little more free to pay my secret calls to the dance hall, which my closeness to him of late had deprived me of.

The rough winds and the brine from the ocean had done their recent work on the entrance to my dance hall. More of the windows was busted. The roof looked like a tent that had billowed and sunk, and lots of big water birds of all kind were circling over the whole edifice. The pines and firs were moving all the time like the winds were inside them, and so many flowers and tufts of grass uprooted by the winds of the past days strewed the ground wherever one stepped. I saw the moon in the sky by daylight, horned and angry and discolored.

But a new strange pith was circulating in my body, a new strength, and looking down at my arms, which had never lost their sinews in all my trouble and absence, I came to with a start. They looked paler, as if the arteries and veins which had moved from within out were deciding to sink back down into my anatomy.

Inside the dance hall nothing had changed however. And one could not hear the winds from within or see the unnatural moon.

I looked through all the victrola records and put on the selection Daventry had played on his harmonica, "On the Alamo."

I was aware night was descending and gradually purpling the ocean, but I felt so strong I danced and danced under the revolving polka-dot ballroom light. I was sick unto death, but there is nothing like dancing to keep one holding to some thread with this world.

I heard the big main entrance door open then, but I did not look round, the record player needed winding, it was ancient, that's why I call it a victrola, it is a victrola. I put on "My Blue Heaven" and danced some more.

I looked up and saw Daventry.

The expression on his face dumbfounded me. I have never seen such a countenance. Oh, if only as they say, one had the power of words, or was a painter, if only—no, no photographer could have caught it either, for the eye sees so many movements and flashes and colors no photo can ever bring—his face, well I knew then he was not human, but a messenger, even his missing teeth was right for his face, which in all the gloom and wind and bad moon shone like spun gold.

I saw the knife in his hand, gleaming, and didn't care, wasn't worried.

"Shan't we die, Garnet, and be rid of this hell, shan't we . . . ?"

"If you say so," I answered him, but a sob escaped me.

"Oh, Garnet," he sighed, "you do so cling to life, poor kid."

He had put the knife to my throat with such force I felt I had already begun to bleed under its cold fine edge.

"We will both die together, in any case, Garnet," he whispered. But as he spoke, I slipped involuntarily from his grasp, so that he had to bring me up again to him and the blade. How odd, I who had lived only with death these four, five years at least, when death was rapping on the portals of my heart, I closed them fast and held to life.

"Whatever you say, Garnet, whatever you wish," I heard him speak, his voice already distant as the storm outside. I heard the knife fall to the bare wood floor.

Then after that terrible embrace, before either of us knew what was happening we were dancing under the shifting many-colored ball that had seen at least a million young girls and boys hold one another as they moved and shifted across the polished floors. Here was a couple the moon had not seen before. I think we were dancers in the grave, or had crossed the great river and left the ferryman and the three-headed Dog far behind. But I was happy again, though it was all so strange, and I wanted to whisper now in his ear to ask him who he was, but what did it matter, someone was holding me again when even the docs had retched and puked at the sight of me, somebody was holding me tight the night before he was to marry my girl.

"You won't leave me now, will you, Daventry?"

He did not answer.

"You mean to leave me." I disengaged myself from him. "You mean to leave me after all that wait and vigil I've had for you."

"That's not so and you know it," he began to reply. "But even should I be called away," and he looked at me in my eyes, which alone now are unharmed by all that happened to me in war, are as bright as anybody's, the whites clear and pure, the blue deep, the pupil inky black and movable as the sun's disc. "Hear me, Garnet," he was going on, looking at me like he was in search of my soul, "I will never leave you even though the firmament part, because we are one, one soul in two tormented halves . . ."

Then he put the pressure of his mouth like a brand on my eyes and lips as if I was soon never to know his presence or touch again . . .

I walked out to the ocean's shore. The sea looked very peculiar, I had never seen it or any other body of water such a color, the height of the waves was tremendous, and the beach was covered with masses of foamy seaweed, dead starfish, rays, and a dead young tern. The sun looked like a cracked brooch such as Mrs. Gondess might wear as a heirloom. From every point of the compass came the cries of warning, from lighthouses, from foghorns, from God knows where: *Go home, go hide, go away, don't linger, clear the beach, run!*

"Oh, Daventry," was all I could say. I knew I had gone mad. I knew I loved him, and not the Widow anymore. And how did I love him? I didn't know because I had never loved a man. I loved him like a mad child loves flame and fire. I wanted to be immolated in his conflagrant blaze.

"Come home, why don't you you, making a fool of yourself!"

"All right for you, Quintus," I answered my reader back. He stood there holding a coat for me to put on.

"Are you comin', Garnet, or am I goin' to have to drag you . . . ?"

My mouth worked to say something, but only spittle came out, which was good because usually even my spit glands don't work. Maybe the coming hurricane was curing them.

"You can thank God I didn't kill your master." Quintus reported Daventry as having made this statement as the sheep rancher's son was packing to leave.

"Ain't that a joke," Quintus went on, "packing when he has about four articles in a paper sack, not counting his socks, and no toothbrush."

I don't know what outraged Quintus more, his (Daventry's) calling me his master, D's offering to murder me for nothing, or his having no belongings to pack, or all of them together.

"Don't you like Daventry by now?" I said after a rest in the conversation. I was back home leafing through a book that Quintus had just finished, some old play written in poetry.

"What are you staring at?" I hear Quintus' voice after a long silent spell rising in alarm.

I looked up from my perusing to study his troubled face.

I put that book away, but he dove for the place in it where I had studied and perused.

I do not have much memory, I can hardly recall my mother's face now, and as I've said in this story of my days, even the daily events fog after an hour of their happening, but the words of that old play, the title of which of course I've lost in disremembrance, were engraved in my brain like electric lights over a movie house:

Behold the lively tincture of his blood!

I began to recite it then to Quintus, I think, as soon as his hand had found my place in the book:

Behold the lively tincture of his blood!
Neither the dropsy nor the jaundice in it,
But the true freshness of a sanguine red,
For all the fog of this black murderous night
Has mixed with it.

I was never sure what happened after that, and even if Quintus had stayed beside me at that climax of catastrophe, I doubt he would be able to recollect it either. I had never had a real quarrel with a black man, and I had never heard words like then come from his throat. I was blamed all upon a sudden, you might say, for all the wrongs committed by one man against another since the dawning of the world, and all this while the hurricane was arriving. He taunted me likewise again and again with having let a murderer take my girl away from me.

I was so confused by Quintus' reproaches, and I had taken so many pills that day, gradually it seemed to me he was the master and had drove me out from my house, I was untenanted, that is, and had no land . . . But though I heard his sorry voice later calling *"Come back, Garnet . . . Come back, Montrose!"* I ran out into the night and into the little woods behind the house, I was on my way to the dance hall, I reckon, when I run across a group of people in outlandish get-up, chanting. I didn't know if I imagined them or not, anyhow I never saw them again after that night, but there about ten to fifteen, all dressed in nightgowns, their heads shaved, and with white paint on their faces, most of them in beads, and yelling some words that couldn't be English. They seized me for a while and asked if I would stay with them and worship their Lord.

I remember telling them about Daventry stealing my girl. They knew all this already, to judge by the expression on their nodding countenances, and they held me tight, which reminded me of how Daventry had danced with me under the revolving dance-hall moon. I knew I was mad then, that my brain had finally suffered the shame and ruin of my body and had likewise turned to the consistency of mulberry wine.

It was at that moment it struck. But it struck again and again, it was all strikes. The firmament parted, to judge by the sickening sound, like all God's handiwork had been throwed down by him in disgust, and the universe smashed to little bits and pieces. I saw, if I can trust to recollection, a whole forest rise and fly into the turbulence, pieces of buildings and bird feathers, clothing and earth, and sheets of water fell and then rose like the ocean had gone up to replace the heavens. There were sounds so terrible I felt my eardrums split, and where the sky had been black as a hundred midnights rushed this new heaven that was the mountain-high sea.

I lay in some hollow where a forest had once been. I was fearful to open my eyes, and fearful not to. I felt my clothes, and for some reason they were not as wet as they should be. Then I looked upwards. There was the sky again, but of course it would never be a real sky again. Its light was coming from too far away, I thought, and was not warmed by the sun I had known. And all around me the teeth of this great wind had left nothing untouched.

"*I don't have too long.*" I remember saying that. I don't know how long I had laid there since I escaped from the band of those shaved-head people in nightgowns. *I don't have too long now*, I kept saying. I was unharmed, it was my mind didn't seem to work now, my body was recovered. I walked straight on because the familiar trees

and cliffs and gently sloping beaches had all been torn
from their sites, and I was walking in a new land.

The first thing I know I was standing in front of Widow
Rance's big house. Save for the ravages about the house
like lost trees and torn up earth, her home stood without a
mark on it. The back screen door was unlatched. I walked
up the steps, each creaking like to be heard a mile away,
and I was already beginning to weep a little, it was the
pills, it was Quintus' cruelty and bitter reproaches, no, I
was mad, that was what, I was mad for I had been sane
too long, like the doc had said long ago, *"Don't hold it all
in, Garnet, tell the world what you feel and keep locked
within, let it all spill out, boy."*

Don't you ever say *boy* to a Virginia white man, I had
replied to the doc.

I stood now in Daventry and Georgina's wedding room,
for now it all rushed back to remembrance. I had, after all,
attended the marriage ceremony at the Grace Evangelical
church, and I pained Georgina, I think, by my quoting
during the service in audible tones from one of those books,
instead of listening to all the preacher said addressing us as
"Dearly beloved," and *"I require and charge you both, as ye
will answer at the dreadful day of judgement,"* and finally
"With this ring I thee wed"—well right over the voice of
the minister I (I remembered now) muttered these profane
but maybe older words picked up from Quintus' voice and
let them be heard in the church, this is what comes of being
a slave to a nigger and hearing things without sense, for I
prophesied aloud:

"Once in Sparta,
at the palace of golden-haired Menelaus,
maidens with bloom of hyacinth in their hair
danced before the new-painted bridal chamber."

"Oh, Garnet, thank God you've come," Georgina was speaking to me now. The wedding, you see, along with the hurricane were past. "Be strong now, won't you?" she admonished when she saw me close my eyes.

"I'll take you to his room." She led me by the arm.

That was a big house that the Widow Rance had, my grandfather's don't compare, and we seemed to walk acres and acres that morning, if it was morning, but of course I kept making her tarry and loiter and say little things, I didn't want to get to his room too soon. I explained also in detail to Widow Rance my fight with Quintus, and that he was leaving me for some high-class black folks in Richmond who had untold wealth, and I told her also how I had been dispossessed, and she was so understanding, though she didn't listen close to what I said.

"You can stay here, Garnet," she kept saying, thinking, I guess, I had no home now. "You're always welcome here, remember that. The welcome mat is always out for a Virginia boy."

But it was too soon! She should have warned me, even if I knowed. It was way too soon.

We stood before this mammoth four-poster bed made from walnut, and there Daventry lay, a little tiny trace of a smile on his face. I think I kept watch on his breast for what seemed like six months. Of course it never raised once, and then I would look at her, and she would nod and smile so sad. A red circle of blood not really dry traced itself around his hairline.

"The undertaker will be here any minute," she said, "and I thank God you have come in time. So look all you care to, on account of you were so close, he told me."

I walked over to the bed and lifted up the sheet and looked at him down to his feet.

"Do you really think he was a sheep-rancher's son?" I inquired.

"If he told you so, I expect."

"Were you very happy?" I inquired.

Georgina was telling me about how it had happened. After the wedding ceremony, they had decided to begin their honeymoon, but the roads were blocked on account of the hurricane warnings, which was supposed to have bypassed our community, but at the last moment there was a radio warning, and an alert, and almost an entire flock of birds was killed and throwed right against the lighthouse and then the hurricane began in earnest.

Georgina had gone inside the house when she realized it had hit.

"It was the wind done it," she said, "a freak wind within the hurricane itself. It lifted Daventry up and carried him to that clump of pitch-pine trees and then just left him standing at the base of the tree trunk, so that when I went in search of him I thought he was just waiting for me, Garnet, but when I went up to him and spoke, I saw he was mashed into that tree as though he belonged in it, and his arms was stretched out as if he would enfold me."

I kept lifting and putting back the sheet, and whether it was the slight breeze created by my raising the sheet or what, his eyes came open and rested on me.

"Do you have any pennies, Georgina?" I said. She had begun to cry then, and she pointed to the bureau where there was some money which had been removed from his pants pockets. I stepped over to the bureau and took up two pennies. I trembled a little, and deposited them on his blue eyes.

The placing of the pennies on his eyelids is the thing, I do believe, that will never leave me out of all the things I have done or had done to me. Why that is I will never know.

Shortly after this Quintus disappeared. I had feared for a long long time that he too was a casualty of the hurricane until one day Edgar Doust drove past to see if I was in need of any produce, and he let out a lot of sly hints based on sly rumors that Quintus had been taken up by some smart rich black people in Richmond whom he had somehow met before but had run into again during the bad storms, and had gone off somewhere with them. I didn't pursue the conversation or ask any information about where this "somewhere" might be, though for all I knew, it might be Africa since he had been threatening to go back there to his homeland, but he knew as well as I that his real homeland and mine is Virginia.

Then I went into the hospital, though there was nothing new wrong with me. I simply asked admission.

But the second or third day after I had been readmitted there, the doc came into my room and then was about to step out again for he thought he had the wrong patient.

"Why, Garnet, is this you?" he inquired after several double takes.

I had known even before Daventry was killed something was changing with me. It was certainly something the doc had never promised. My appearance of having been turned to mulberry wine, actually my appearance of having been massacred and yet left among the living had been changing ever since Daventry had arrived. I will always look horrible, of course, but now instead of a massacred man—and this is what the doc took in immediately—I look in his words merely like a man that has been in a boxing match every day for five years without stopping. So even now the few times I go to a strange place people will say or whisper behind my back, *"What do you suppose the other fellow looks like?"* A kind of standard joke around here.

Winter came, most of the birds had left except the chickadees, and it was colder and rawer than I ever remembered

it. Sometimes in those long-drawn-out evenings I would go
to the hall mirror and study myself. To tell the honest
truth I think I look worse now that I have turned back into
resembling any Virginia white man who gets beat up frequently to someone I do not know. But it is no even slight
exaggeration to say that I have come back from another
world.

I was thinking then of putting more ads in the newspaper
and interviewing new applicants, but when you have met
the real applicant, and if you count Quintus also and say
applicants, then why have any more? I read those hard
deep books also between whiles occasionally, but all the
pith and substance has gone out of them. Like today I
picked up a tome at random and read,

> They used no images to represent the object of their
> worship, nor did they meet in temples or buildings
> of any kind for the performance of their sacred rites.
> A circle of stones constituted their sacred place, situ-
> ated near some stream or under the shadow of a grove
> or wide-spreading oak.

I thought of the ruined dance hall, and could not wait to
get my togs on and visit there. Why had I not gone sooner?
Yes, for it was all that was left, all that would ever partly
satisfy my longing.

I hurried up the cliff, but at the top, my stay in the hospital having made me soft, I sort of gave out, losing my
breath, but I got up again and then ran all the way. I decided once I got inside all would be revealed, all would be

known forever and ever. I felt he would come and explain everything.

But it was a pretty sorry mess inside. The great revolving moon was gone with its polka-dot lights, and the piano was busted, together with the bandstand, innocent victims of the hurricane and the flood of rain concomitant with it.

I stood a long time weeping, for my lachrymal glands have come back to normal along with my complexion. Then my eye, still swimming, spied with some difficulty the old victrola. I went over to it, and wound it up. "On the Alamo" was already on the turntable, and I set the motor to going.

I was dancing all by myself, as happy as one who had lost everything, even the stain of his horror, could be, when I heard the big front door open. Then steps. I dared not turn round, I dared not stop dancing, and the music sounded so pitifully far-off and thin, so old-fashioned and vanished, and long ago with its words about garden gates and moonlight and roses and love's dream being o'er. My new tears had also blinded me, so there was no point even trying to see who had come in, but I felt a gentle hand on the nape of my neck.

"Daventry?" I inquired.

"No, it's just me, Garnet," the voice said.

I turned then to look and it was of course her, who else?

She had put her arms about me, I had never quit dancing anyhow, and we moved off into the center part of the circular ballroom with the music reaching us fainter and fainter.

The record stopped, and we stopped. We looked into one another's eyes.

"So you knew my secret all the time then too, along with him?" I said.

All of a sudden the music started again, the same number, and we stood hardly moving our feet at all, but holding one another, the way you hold people in dreams you don't want to go on holding, and at the same time you can't let go. I smelled her favorite heliotrope perfume and there was never any skin like hers, if snow was warm it would be Georgina, Daventry's skin might have looked fresher, but it was not soft as falling snow.

The droll thing about getting what you long for is the longing was better, longing pains more, but it's more what you want. I had just walked away from Georgina leaving her under the ruined polka-dot moon and the orchestra doing "On the Alamo" for the twentieth time. I hardly knew I had left her.

The tables were turned then, but their turning bored me more than they vindicated me. They were, though, turned completely. I had tried to tell the doc about my feelings, that is, that at first I had loved Georgina, childhood sweetheart, etc., and now I was in love with this son of a sheep-rancher from Utah who had been killed in the hurricane. The doc smiled and nodded and listened. He would always let me say anything, I guess, but he never said much back, but this time he said something vague, like all human feelings, you see, are as old as history. As if I cared about history or it was any use to me.

I missed Quintus almost more than Daventry because as long as he was sitting around reading, and sharing his learning with me, why the very irritation of his presence, his peevishness, the fact that he hated me even maybe (I guess he hated me), all made me feel at home with him, for there is nobody more Virginian than Quintus. Daventry had become my permanent secret like the ruined dance hall, but Quintus was home, and so I missed him fearfully, but would have bit my tongue off rather than say it.

Then she got her "applicants." That took the place of me being irritated and riled up and puzzled and half-entertained by Quintus and his old reading texts.

Her applicants were young men who had been children when I was fighting for my country.

They came in the morning and sometimes again in the P.M. with a letter signed always "Your Georgina."

I could tell of course they were all—the letters—imitated from Daventry and even me, and here now I had taken Georgina's place in the scheme of events. I no longer loved her. I would go and look at myself in the mirror, I sort of looked normal now except I reminded myself of the man in the nursery rhyme who had scratched out both his eyes in a quickset hedge and then jumped into another hedge and scratched them in again.

A young man came one forenoon with a larger than

usual letter, to judge by the envelope, and I embarrassed him greatly by asking him to read the contents. He looked about fourteen, the down was just showing on his cheeks but not really on his upper lip.

All the time though while he read the letter I was thinking about how I didn't even have a snapshot of Daventry. The only thing I had from him to prove he even ever existed was a bandana handkerchief and I kept it under my pillow.

"Would you mind reading the letter again?" I said, for I realized that all the time he had been droning out what she had penned I hadn't heard a syllable.

The boy's chin trembled, but I gather she must have paid him good, for he swallowed his choler and began to read it all over again:

"What can I say to convince you that it has been you all along that I have cared for . . . When you came home from the war it was not that I rejected you, I suffered I do believe more from what had happened to you than you yourself . . ."

I don't recollect all she said and having the boy read it a second time didn't keep my mind on it successively, so I missed several paragraphs. In fact he could have read it over and again until the Last Judgment, I wouldn't have heard it all, for my mind was on other things, and I was also looking in the mirror at myself most of the time he was reading, so at least hearing the silence that came from his final delivery, I turned to him, and give him a fifty-cent piece for his pains.

The thing I had been looking at in the mirror while he read was this, my face was no longer anywhere the color of mulberry.

That was the longest and coldest winter I ever remember, the very tears froze on one's face. Even the ocean acted funny, like it was sulking, though I listened to it now more than before, before him, that is, before the one I love, for it had bothered him, the wind, and the ocean he was critical of, whereas I had always taken them for granted, but that long winter I am talking about when I was alone, when I had changed from the color of mulberry back to my white Virginia winter face, it seemed to me that the ocean was complaining, rather than angry, that it whimpered and sobbed and talked to itself in its sleep, that it digged and delved like it was looking for Daventry too, who is buried nearby in a Confederate cemetery, which I don't know would please him, but we didn't have any idea where to send him in Utah, and the Widow tends his grave, and when good weather comes, we will bring fresh flowers to it, you can count on that.

But spring did come finally, and I found in one of Quintus' tomes some lines I did prize, see if I can recollect them right:

The blossom is the token of the rebirth of the year, it
is the trees' rejoicing. It is then that trees show themselves new creatures and are transformed from what
they really are, and quite revel in rivaling each other
with their varied hues of coloring.

I was pretending to read one night late, for I had been
in some pain in my chest, I was reading as usual in some
ancient book about a place once called Arabia Felix, when
I hear a kind of banging at the garden gate. The goose-
pimples came over me like a sheet of ice had been slipped
down over the base of my spine.

Then I heard a soft knock. I don't think I would have
ever gone to the door had whoever it was not been so patient, that is he sort of went on drumming on the wood,
like a bird, and I knew he would never let up until I went
out and let him in.

I didn't know him at all. It was his clothes that threw
me off. He was dressed like some old-time swell, gold
watchchain, cuff links, tie clasp, big parrotlike showy tie,
hand-sewn lapels, flashy high shoes, oh you name it.

He streaks in and rushes to the kitchen and took down a
glass and was drinking some water from the hydrant without so much as hello, kissmyass, or what have you.

I was gasping with rage and terror, but then I looked
again and who of course was it but Quintus, but transformed like he had been touched by a wand, in fact I
looked around to see if he didn't have any retinue of
followers.

"Why didn't you speak?" I began my wrangling, but then after a moment I felt too good to be mad, and I sat down beside him there in the kitchen.

My eyes were riveted to his fingers, for there they sparkled, diamond and precious gem rings, or so they seemed.

"Did you have a rich uncle or somebody die?" I had begun my interrogatory, but he held up his fingers to be silent.

"I couldn't pay the price anymore, Garnet."

That "Garnet" sounded so good, for he said it as only a Virginian can say it, and I gave out two short sobs before I could control myself.

"These rich black people from Richmond I met during the hurricane offered to take me to Mexico." He began a long narrative, which like the Widow's applicant letters to me, did not hold my undivided attention. So I did not and do not recollect any more of what he done or had done to him than phrases like *all they wanted was sex . . . my peter . . . money . . . they drunk so damn much . . . tequila can kill a man . . .*

Then there was a long long talk again like his reading to me, about the Aztec ruins and Chapultepec and another city that had a church built in it for every day in the year and blinded you with its white domes in the sun . . .

"So you come home, then, did you?" I begun on him in earnest at last. "And you expected the door to be open wide, did you, and the welcome mat still out?"

"I did hear one thing in town, before I come back,"

Quintus spoke somewhat uneasy like. "That the Widow Rance has asked your hand in marriage . . ."

I grinned then in spite of myself.

"So," I chose my own words carefully, "are you home to stay, Quintus, after this sex and tequila spree in Old Mexico . . . or did you just come past to crow over me in all your riches and splendor . . . ?"

"I know where I belong," Quintus began again, "but I ain't told you why I come back, you see."

"I thought it was 'cause you got tired of sex, you said."

"*One night,*" he began, and again it was like the old days when he would recite to me out of the hard books whose long crawling sentences and tales of times and deeds so long forgotten make the mind pain and slow down, he spoke of a garden fragrant with jasmine in this Old Mexico town where he had gone. "*One night I had taken a seat in an antique carved chair, and whether it was the fragrance of the strange flowers or what, I looked up and seen . . . Daventry . . .*"

I buried my head in my hands.

"*It was him all right,*" Quintus went on implacable, "*just like he looked in life, Garnet.*"

I covered my ears then too, but his words rung through to my brain and hammered there.

"*He said to me, 'Go home, Quintus, for he needs you, go home at once . . .'*"

There was this prolonged cessation of talk then during which only the water hydrant dripped, which has needed fixing with a new washer for a year or more.

———————————

I brought my eyes to the level of his eyes after a while, and my face must have been as red as when it was the stain of mulberry, and I said, "And did you just obey him or was there some small part of you wanted to come home?"

"Well," Quintus replied, taking off his new jacket and the gold tie and clasp, "after all, I am as you always say a Virginia boy, and I thought I'd stay with you until your wedding with the Widow takes place at least . . ."

"That'll be a long stay, then, Quints . . . Did you hear in town too how she has applicants and sends them here with letters to be read to me, just like the position I was in once . . . ?"

I heard Quintus' old laugh then, and I almost laughed myself, but stopped . . .

"*I wonder why he never has appeared to me, Quintus,*" I started up, going back to his having seen the apparition in Mexico . . . "*When I wanted it so . . . When . . .*"

"Well," Quintus spoke, eyeing me a little concernedly, but taking off his shoes and rubbing his own feet now, "maybe, Garnet, it's because he figures he's with you all the time anyhow . . ."

"Oh, I see," I said hopefully. "Well maybe that's the way it has to be after all."

The screen door moved under the April breeze, and I could just visualize the first peach blossoms that would be coming out in not too many days, and I took another look at Quintus' togs and his big gold watch with the chain spread over his broad chest. I listened then also to hear if the ocean would make any kind of comment on the prodigal's return, but no matter how I pricked up my ears, as Quintus went off into his own part of the house to turn in, strain as I would I couldn't hear another sound at all of any kind outside. Of course it was terrible late, and calm this time of night, and the last of the bad weather was past.